Battle Ready

Equipping and Encouraging the Teens in God's Army

by J.E. Solinski

The BELT of TRUTH

Battle Ready

by J.E. Solinski

Scripture quotations taken from the New American Standard Bible® Copyright © 1960, 1962, 1963,1968, 1971, 1972, 1973, 1975, 1977, 1995 by the Lockman Foundation. Used by permission. (www.Lockman.org)

ISBN: 978-0-9989096-2-2(sc)
Library of Congress Control Number: 2018952390

Second Edition
July 2025

AMOC PUBLICATIONS™

To all my students over the years.
I have drawn from your experiences and your hearts.

Note to Reader

The stories in this collection span twenty-five years of writing. Therefore, many of the stories won't have cell phones or computers or other current technology. While some struggles are unique to a certain generation because of the technology or the lack of it, most of the challenges the teens in these stories face are common to all generations. I hope you enjoy them and take away a kernel of truth from each one.

Therefore put on the full armor of God, so that
when the day of evil comes, you may be able to stand
your ground, and after you have done everything, to
stand. ¹⁴ Stand firm then, with

the belt of truth

buckled around your waist, with the breastplate of righteousness in place, ¹⁵ and with your feet fitted with the
readiness that comes from the gospel of peace.
¹⁶ In addition to all this, take up the shield of faith,
with which you can extinguish all the flaming arrows
of the evil one. ¹⁷ Take the helmet of salvation and the
sword of the Spirit, which is the word of God.
(Ephesians 6:13–17)

Table of Contents

Learning to Lead

Greg Harris finished lacing up his shoes, then rubbed the palms of his hands up his socks. He picked up the basketball lying next to him, stood up, and tested each shoe on the gym floor.

Satisfied with the fit, he spun the basketball on his finger as he walked toward the basket. Fifteen feet away, he dribbled twice, faked out an imaginary opponent, and then let loose a jumper which swished through the net cords.

Greg smiled with satisfaction. He loved basketball, and he was good at it. Last year, he was the only junior starter on the championship team and he'd been second highest scorer. Now as a senior, he had hopes of being named Most Valuable and perhaps League Player of the Year. But the smile quickly faded as he jogged to retrieve the ball. Not much chance of that the way things were going. This team was young. Though there were three other returning seniors, none of them had seen much playing time last year. The remainder of the team was juniors up from a rather pathetic junior varsity team.

Coach Leonard had singled him out before the start of the season and impressed upon him the importance of his leadership. To take charge and help bring this young team along.

Well, he'd tried. Practice had been going for two weeks now and besides always being first on the floor for practice, he had fought for every rebound and driven the basket or shot every chance he had. Defensively, he'd tried to cover even more than his area. He was all over the court. But it didn't seem to be making much difference. In fact, it had only brought a reprimand from the coach. "Pass more," he instructed. "Take care of your man. Keep your position." It irritated Greg to even think about it now What did the guy want? He tells me to be a leader, and then he tells me not to do anything.

He took aim at the basket and shot. The ball careened off the side of the rim, and Greg walked after it. He was frustrated, and when he was frustrated, his whole game suffered.

The other guys were just now coming into the gym, joking around, grabbing balls, and shooting. Greg didn't say anything to them, and they returned his silence. For the past two weeks he had dressed quickly and come to the gym early. He had foregone their locker room revelry to show them how seriously he took the game, but they had taken little notice. How can a guy lead if they won't follow? he wondered.

The shrill blast of a whistle destroyed his thoughts.

"Everybody over here!" yelled Coach Leonard.

Greg tucked the ball under his arm and trotted to where the others were huddling.

"Listen up," Coach Leonard began sharply. "We have our first practice game next Tuesday, and frankly, I don't think we're ready." He paused and looked directly at each player. "We lack teamwork," he continued still drilling individuals with his stare, "and proper leadership." His eyes rested on Greg. Greg shifted his weight.

Come on, he thought. What do you want?

"We're going to start practice with an intra-squad scrimmage. Moebes, Harris, Cook, Montgomery, Rhoades—you're gold, and…"

Greg reversed his practice jersey and jogged out to position himself on the court not waiting for the others. Alright, he vowed to himself, if he wants leadership, he'll get it.

For fifteen minutes Greg dominated play but still his team couldn't get on track. They missed easy shots, threw the ball away, and were disorganized on defense. Greg's frustration became visible. Finally, Coach blew the whistle, and the same frustration was written on his face. Greg nodded in agreement. Now he knows how I feel, he thought.

"Harris! Take a seat for a while. Jenkins! Go to gold. Sykes! Blue."

Greg jogged to the bench, glad for the breather. He

leaned back and watched the others, but what he saw was not pleasing. Slowly they were getting their rhythm, playing as a team, and looking much better than when he was out there. Greg glanced at Coach Leonard and realized that he had made the same discovery. Greg sulked on the sideline until it came time to drill, and then he continued to dwell on this unsettling revelation. After practice, he showered and quickly left, glad for the weekend. He needed some distance to relax, but he couldn't keep his mind off basketball.

Saturday, he shot baskets, honing his skills. Sunday, as he sat in Sunday school class, he tried to put a finger on the intangible problem of the team. He didn't hear a word of the lesson and afterward walked into the sanctuary to find his parents for church. He was still lost in his own thoughts when the minister's words broke his concentration.

"'You know that the rulers of the Gentiles lord over them, and their great men exercise authority over them,'" he quoted. "'It is not so among you, but whosoever wishes to become great among you shall be your servant, and whoever wishes to be first among you shall be your slave: just as the Son of Man did not come to be served, but to serve, and to give His life...'"

Greg sat stunned. That's not true, he reasoned. Thousands of people followed Christ, never leaving Him alone. His disciples hung on every word. They counted on Him. He was a leader!

But as he listened intently to the sermon, he realized that Christ was a servant. He served the people he came to lead: from washing their feet, to feeding and healing them, to dying for them.

Monday afternoon as he walked to the gym, he was filled with nervous anticipation. He took a deep breath, swallowed his pride, and entered the locker room. The other guys were already changing and exchanging good-natured ribbing. They didn't try to include Greg; he hadn't expected they would. He dressed quickly and went to the gym, but this time he didn't start shooting. Instead he waited next to the ball bag. Soon the others came in.

"Here you go, Jim!" he yelled and tossed Jim a ball. Caught totally by surprise, Jim almost let the ball smack him in the face but managed to get his hands up.

"Don!" Greg yelled and tossed another one.

"Thanks," Don mumbled and looked at him strangely. Greg tried not to notice. He continued tossing balls and singling out individual players. Coach Leonard soon arrived wearing the same weary look he had left with on Friday. After an hour of drilling, Coach called for a fifteen minute scrimmage.

"Moebes, Rhoades, Cook, Montgomery…" He paused as his eyes surveyed the squad before resting on Greg. Greg held his breath and kept his eyes on the ground, praying hard.

"Harris!" he barked. "You guys go gold."

Greg let out a sigh. "Thank you, Lord," he whispered. The others were already on the floor, and Greg hustled to take his position. The ball was tossed and the tip went to Greg. He had a clear lane to the basket but saw that Jim had already broken down court. He passed to him. It caught Jim completely by surprise, but he still laid it up for two points.

"Nice shot," Greg commented.

"Thanks," Jim replied and looked at him strangely.

Greg pretended not to notice and hustled down court to set up on defense. For ten minutes he set up plays, faked shots, and passed off, congratulated and encouraged, while his teammates played in stunned silence. Finally, however, they accepted Greg's new role, loosened up, and enjoyed themselves. The change was radically noticeable. Confidence began to surface, and the five gold players began to work with uncanny synchronized precision. Coach Leonard let the scrimmage run the entire hour only stopping to address minor problems.

When he blew his whistle to end practice, the smile on his face matched the obvious joy of the players. A couple of the guys slapped Greg on the back, and he returned the gesture before heading toward the locker room.

"Hey Harris!"

Greg stopped and noticed Coach Leonard motioning him over. He jogged back. Coach Leonard was rubbing his face and studying the ground. He sucked in his lower lip and looked up at Greg.

"What happened out there, Harris?" he questioned, watching Greg closely.

Greg became suddenly concerned. "Was everything OK, Coach? I mean, did I do anything wrong?" he asked.

"Wrong? No," Coach Leonard replied. "I'd say you did everything right. I just wanted to know why. Why the sudden change?"

Greg breathed a sigh of relief, smiled, and shook his head. "Let's just say I'm learning to lead, Coach," he replied. And then he turned and headed for the showers.

Valentine's Card

Jeremy stared at the array of cards before him and felt his palms grow sweaty. What was he going to do? There had to be over two hundred cards here to choose from, and it was all important that he pick exactly the right card for Krista.

Just the thought of her made him smile. They had been going out for only a little over a month, so this was the first time he'd had to buy anything for her, and he had to buy something for her, but what a mess a guy could find himself in if he didn't pick the right card.

He picked up one from the rack and read it.

Roses are red,

Violets are blue.

So what else is new?

Happy Valentine's Day.

Pretty clever, but he didn't think Krista would think it was that great of a card. Too corny and, well, Valentine's Day was supposed to have a little more feeling in it. He tried another.

On this Valentine's Day,

I want to give you what I know your heart most desires.

He opened the card and looked inside.

A picture of me! Happy Valentine's Day!

He grinned. It had possibilities, but seemed a bit egotistical. And they didn't know each other that well. She might think he was being serious. He put it back and moved down the row to the cards that looked a little more serious. He picked one up. It had two pages of gushing verse, and he felt his feet go cold and his fingers numb. Hurriedly he stuck it back. A card like that could wind up getting a guy married. No thank you.

He ran his finger around his collar and dove back in. This was murder. They should have a little manual out there for guys on how to pick the right card. If you pick one too romantic, she thinks you proposed. Pick one too casual, you've lost her to the competition. It was worse than buying roses. At least with roses you knew where you stood. White means friendship and red, love. Simple. But not cards.

"Excuse me," he apologized when he bumped into another guy searching through the racks. He looked around. There were tons of guys just like him, perusing through the cards with anguish, searching for that perfect card. He hit an entire empty shelf.

Guess I shouldn't have waited until Valentine's Day to do this, he chastised himself. He figured the perfect card for Krista had probably been in that now barren bank of shelves right in front of him. Now he was left with all the losers—well, he and the other fifty guys here who had waited until the last minute.

Girls have it easy, he thought. Guys don't even read the cards they buy, or if they do, they don't really take them seriously—though you'd better look like you read it and enjoyed it in front of her. But girls, man, they pour over every card, reading each verse as though it was written just for them. And then they give you those eyes that tell you you either went too far and now were in hot water, didn't go far enough and were in hot water, or—he thought about it for a moment. Maybe you never win. Maybe there were no perfect cards. Maybe the card industry knew this and just set men up for the kill.

He rubbed his eyes and looked at his watch. He was supposed to pick Krista up in a little over two hours, and here he was still in the card shop. He closed his eyes and prayed.

Lord, if ever I needed your help, it's now. Please help me pick out the perfect card.

He moved along the rack and grabbed one, knowing full well this was not truly a godly approach. He looked at the front. A cute little puppy with a forlorn look. That was good. It was cute. Girls were into cute. It wasn't overly romantic. Guys don't like overly romantic. He opened it up.

I'd be lost without you as my Valentine.

Happy Valentine's Day!

OK, he thought. It was a little sentimental, but it wasn't overkill. Plus, it was short. Those long ones could get a guy into too much trouble.

He breathed a sigh of relief and headed for the counter, then grabbed a box of candy on the way. What the heck. He was feeling pretty good now. He paid the cashier and went whistling down the mall.

What was it about these holidays? Three hundred and sixty-two days of the year, he didn't have to worry about little problems like these, the sticky situations. But Christmas, birthdays, and Valentine's Day a guy could find himself in a tight pickle without some guidance. He should probably pay more attention to all the signals girls send during the rest of the year, listen to his mother's advice, and watch more of those informational news shows with Connie Chung or Barbara Walters that come right before such holidays.

He tilted his head in thought. It was a lot like his Christian walk now that he thought about it. He really didn't think much about God's principles for most of the year because life just kind of cruised along without any major hiccups. But when he *did* find himself in a tight spot, in unfamiliar terrain, it certainly did help to have some very clear guidelines to help him through.

He sobered. How many times had he balked at God's principles, squirmed under their seeming narrowness? How many times had he really wanted to tune out the sermon or the lesson? He was thankful now that he hadn't. It was one thing messing up a relationship with a girl you had known for a month because you made a social blunder. But it was something else to jeopardize your relationship with God because of a moral one.

Miracle of Miracles

The ground was soft and warm. That meant Dad, Kevin, and I were out behind the house getting the garden plot ready for spring planting. Dad's a farmer, and before he ever plants the main fields, he, Kevin, and I prepare the family garden plot by hand so that it's ready for Mom.

"Got to keep our perspective," he always said, though I never really knew what he meant by that.

This year, the first weekend in March was pleasant enough. Dad pulled out the hoes and rakes, fertilizers, trowels, and whatnot. He then came in to help Mom cook a sizable breakfast before herding us out to the overgrown patch of ground and manning us with our weapons. I drew first blood with the cultivator, Kevin attacked with a hoe, and Dad took after the larger enemy camps with a shovel.

None of us said much at first. The air was cool enough that we could still see our breath, so we worked hard just to warm up. When the sun did finally begin working its warmth, Kevin rose from his task and looked over the eighth acre of land.

"Doesn't seem like we've made much headway," he said sadly, taking in the meager row of weeds he had laid to waste behind him. I glanced over my trail of battered bodies and could claim only about two more feet worth of victory.

"Never does," I said and went back to my task while Dad straightened up.

"Don't look at what lies ahead," he said, "nor what lays waste behind. Just focus on the task before you, and you'll be more than fine."

I had to grin. Put Dad in a field with dirt up to his armpits and he waxes philosophic and poetic every time. And usually his advice rings true. I bent my back deeper into my work and began to let my mind drift, but not Kevin. It may take him a while to wake up, but once he does, there's really no shutting him up.

"Hey, guess what?" he said and then didn't wait for any acknowledgment. "Darrel's mom was diagnosed with cancer almost two months ago, and when they went in last week for Xrays, the doctors couldn't find a trace of the stuff. Pretty weird, huh?"

"Sounds to me like someone made a mistake the first time," I said, continuing my hacking and hoping Kevin would get the hint.

"Huh-uh," he retorted. "Darrel said his family asked for

a copy of both Xrays, and you can't deny it. On the first one there were all kinds of something in her lungs and in the second not a speck."

"Must have been faulty equipment then," I countered. "A person can't have lungs full of cancer one day and then nothing the next."

"Why not?"

The question came from my dad, not Kevin, and it caught us both off guard.

"Well, because it doesn't make sense," I said.

"Don't you believe God can heal people?" he probed.

"That's it too," Kevin added excitedly. "After the first Xray, Darrel and his family met with the elders of their church and they, what do you call it, laid hands on his mom and prayed. She said she felt this warm feeling all through her body and then—*voila*—the next time she was cured."

Dad turned to look at me.

"Well, Ryan. Don't you think that can happen?" he asked.

I felt put on the spot. I had only entered this conversation out of courtesy to Kevin so that he didn't feel as if he were talking to the dirt, and now *I* was on trial.

"I don't know. I mean, you hear about all these guys claiming to be able to heal people and then they turn out to be charlatans."

"I didn't ask about all these people. I asked if you

thought *God* could heal people."

"Sure. Jesus did it in the Bible."

"Do you think He can still heal people?"

"Well . . . sure."

"Do you think He can cure people through other people as He did with the disciples?"

I felt uncomfortable. Dad was using one of those argumentative techniques that backed you right into a very small corner.

"I guess so," I said in my most non-committal voice.

"Then why don't you think Darrel's mother was cured?"

I was really squirming for a credible answer now.

"Because it just doesn't make sense. Cancer is a deadly disease. People don't just get over it."

"So God only cures colds and flu and stuff like that?"

This really isn't fair, I thought.

"Well, He doesn't do it all the time," I said.

"I see," his father said and started in on his shoveling again. I wondered if that was the abrupt end of the conversation. It wasn't.

"How many times did God part the Red Sea?" Dad asked.

Now where did that come from? I wondered. *Was it a trick question?*

"Once as far as I know."

"So does that mean God didn't do it because He didn't

do it more than once?" he asked.

"Of course not," I said, feeling that Dad was being unnecessarily petty. Kevin saw his chance to rejoin the conversation and jumped in excitedly.

"Did you know that some scientists believe the parting of the Red Sea was caused by a strong wind that blew across the land, holding the sea back on one side? Then there was this kind of shelf on the other side that kept that water back, or something like that. Billy was telling me about it."

I stared at him incredulously.

"So what does that mean? That God didn't do it? That it was just some act of nature?" I asked. Now whose side was I on?

Kevin just shrugged. He figured the revelation was enough in itself.

"Well, that's what some people would like us to believe," his father said. "Don't get me wrong. I'm not saying that that's not how it happened. God is in charge of nature, and He can work His wonders in any fashion. But beware of men trying to explain away the unexplainable."

"Why wouldn't God just do something outright, so that there can't be any questions raised?" I asked.

Dad's eyebrows rose.

"There will always be questions," he said. "Who's to say that Darrel's mother wasn't healed outright? Yet you asked questions and made statements trying to explain it away, and you're a Christian who claims to believe in miracles."

I thought about that a moment. "I guess I find it easier to believe in miracles that happened in some other time than those that happen now."

Dad nodded. "Exactly. Even as Jesus was performing His miracles, many did not believe. It is man's basic nature to be skeptical and disbelieving. If he can't understand it with his finite little mind, then he just doesn't think it's possible."

Dad picked up his shovel and moved over to where Kevin and I stood.

"I know it's hard to believe in miracles such as instantaneous healing and exorcising demons. We live, and man has always lived, in a world that lies, perverts, and distorts the truth, then manipulates it for its own end. No wonder man is skeptical. No wonder it takes an act of faith to believe."

He paused and pointed to a tiny shoot near the toe of my shoe. It had somehow survived the winter and was struggling to make a new life in the cold ground.

"But when I look at a new plant growing or a baby lamb just out of his mother's womb, or the beauty of God's earth in the morning light..." and he stretched his arm over the expanse of earth and sky and distant mountains. "When I see all that, well, that's miracle enough for me to know that Jesus is indeed Lord of all."

Check

Michelle stared at the board, viewing the situation at hand. After evaluating her opponent's options and probable next few moves, she moved her queen's bishop. By the way Jerry's mouth dropped, it was obviously not an expected move.

"Check," Michelle said.

"What –"

"Check," Michelle repeated with a smug grin on her face.

"I see that," Jerry said as he narrowed his eyes and looked the board over intently.

"Careful, you'll burn holes in the board, and then we won't be able to play any more," Michelle quipped. But Jerry ignored her, and Michelle could tell by the way his eyes were hopping all over the place that he was playing about five moves ahead. Suddenly, his worried expression was replaced by one of confidence, and he moved his knight to protect.

Michelle pursed her lips. She hadn't seen that defense. She couldn't just move in with her bishop, because a pawn was sitting there ready to snatch it up. A knight for a bishop. She didn't think so. Some experts advocated sacrificing pieces, but Michelle wasn't into sacrificing. She was into hoarding.

She looked her options over and then saw an opening. Her heart quickened. She moved her queen. Two more moves and she could have Jerry in checkmate. She leaned back to relax and looked across at him. She enjoyed watching him squirm.

Only he wasn't squirming. He was trying hard to hold back a smile of satisfaction. It took him no time to move his next piece.

"Check," he said. Michelle stared at her vulnerable king and realized what she had done. When she had moved her queen, she had left her king unprotected. Now she was on the defense. She studied the board for what seemed like hours, looking for possibilities. But there was only one—pull back. She did, and Jerry, without a second thought, moved his own queen into position.

"Check!" he said again, with too much enthusiasm for Michelle's liking.

Again, there was only one place to move and that was back.

"Check!" Jerry yelled. "And mate!"

Michelle stared at the pathetic scene before her. It was

true. She was dead. She turned her king over in submission and heaved a heavy sigh. What did she expect? It had been a bad day all around. Make that a bad week.

"Want to play again?" Jerry asked enthusiastically as he started re-setting the board.

"You've got to be kidding," Michelle said. "By the way, when did you suddenly get so good?"

Jerry grinned. "I've been reading up on strategies."

"Sounds exciting," she mumbled. "No life, huh?"

Jerry winced. Michelle knew it was a low blow, and she was sorry she said it. But she didn't feel like apologizing.

"I've got a life," Jerry said.

"Sorry," Michelle answered. It was easier to apologize than hear Jerry correct her on the status of his existence. Besides, he was a useful neighbor to have around. Two years her younger, he still had a crush on her. But it wasn't as bad as it once was, and if she kept berating him, he would be cured of it all together.

"Besides, if I want to get better," he continued, "I have to know some strategies so I can tell what other people are trying on me."

Michelle nodded apathetically. She'd had enough. She needed a breather.

"I didn't mean anything by it," she said. "I've just had a lousy day. I think I'd better get going anyway. Thanks for the game."

"Anytime," Jerry responded as he walked her to the

door. She could tell he meant it. She hadn't killed his good nature with her comments after all.

Though October was just around the corner, the air was still summer warm. She headed down the street toward her house, but when she hit the park, she made a left turn. She was depressed and could use a good walk.

Her life had been going great until this year. Then everything went haywire, and she didn't know what to do. What was worse was that she was a Christian but was finding no solace or solutions in her faith. Wasn't this where it was all supposed to pay off? Wasn't this when Jesus and God were supposed to put it into high gear and pull off a few miracles? What was she supposed to do? She tried to remember what she had learned in Sunday school. One verse popped into her mind.

But seek first his kingdom and his righteousness, and all these things will be given to you as well.

She thought about it for a moment. The ending was nice —"all these things will be given to you as well." If by "all these things" God meant Todd, her old boyfriend, liking her again and her grades picking up and finding a job, then she was all for it. But the first part stumped her. What did it mean to seek the kingdom of God? What was she supposed to do?

It was probably spelled out in the Bible, but Michelle realized she knew very little about the Bible. Oh, she had read a lot of it, but without paying too much attention.

She knew all the major stories and a multitude (well, a mouthful) of verses but never paid attention to what they were actually saying.

She turned and began to walk quickly. She needed to get home. She felt a hunger, a real thirst, for what was in the Bible. Suddenly the verse "as the deer pants for streams of water, so my soul pants for you, O God" made sense. She couldn't get home fast enough.

Michelle let the door slam behind her and then winced, waiting for the reprimand.

"Michelle!"

"Sorry, Mom, I forgot."

She hurried to her room and pulled out her Bible. Where should she start? There was so much. Yesterday, the thought of reading through the entire Bible would have seemed like a monumental task. Today, it seemed just as overwhelming but very exciting. She started looking at all the passages she had highlighted over the years.

"Be still, and know that I am God…" That was Psalm 46:10. She read it again, placing her own emphasis.

"Be *still*, and know that I am God…" She had a tough time doing nothing. For one, she wanted to run back to Todd and grovel, but she knew she shouldn't. You couldn't make someone like you.

"Be still, and know that *I* am God…" Now that was appropriate for her. How many times did she think that *she* was God, taking matters into her own hands?

"Be still, and know that I am *God…*" Even more appropriate. Why worry? God is infinitely powerful.

She skimmed the pages again. That was only one portion of one verse, and look how much could be drawn from it. She found another.

"Blessed is the one who waits…" There was that awful "waiting" again. She was pretty sure that the more she read the more that little theme would materialize.

"Now to him who is able to do immeasurably more than all we ask or imagine" (Ephesians 3:20). Michelle stared at this for awhile in surprise. How many times had she read it without realizing its meaning? The things she wanted, the things she asked for, were pretty petty, and He was able to do "immeasurably more" if she'd only let Him.

She shook her head. Four verses out of an ocean of promises. Why had she stayed away? What blessings had she been missing? What footholds had Satan found?

She needed to read more so she could equip herself against Satan and become better acquainted with the God she claimed to "trust." She let out a sigh. When had she ever needed to trust? You don't need to trust when everything is sailing smoothly. But when the rough water comes… . She picked up her Bible and started gleaning the bits left behind from younger years. Suddenly Jerry's delving into books to develop his chess strategies didn't seem so silly. It seemed infinitely wise. It was a good thing God had allowed her to be put in "check."

Golf Lesson

"This is why Mark Twain said golf 'was a good walk spoiled.'"

The four boys laughed and just looked at the golf ball wedged between two rocks in the hazard.

"So is it one club length or two from the red stakes?" Morgan, the owner of the ball, asked.

"Two."

"You sure?"

"Yup. Here I'll show you."

Kyle grabbed Morgan's driver from his golf bag.

"So you are calling an unplayable, right?" he asked.

"Yeah," replied Morgan. "So now I have to take a drop, right, and a one stroke penalty?"

"Right on both counts. Two club lengths from where it entered the hazard on the same line and no closer to the hole."

"But I'm not going to use my driver to hit it," Morgan said, seeing Kyle with his club.

"I know," Kyle replied, "but you can use your longest club to determine your drop." He then proceeded to show Morgan how to drop his club, mark the first club length with a tee, then drop the club again, mark the second club length, and then stand and drop his ball from shoulder height.

"Now you're ready to hit."

"Thanks, Kyle," Morgan said. "Sorry, guys," he yelled to the other two in the foursome who were watching and waiting.

"No problem," came the replies, almost in unison. "That's why we practice together."

Morgan pulled his five wood from his bag, took a deep breath, took a couple of practice swings, lined up his shot, and swung. The ball sailed through the air, landed just short of the green, and rolled toward the hole, stopping four feet from the pin.

"Woo hoo!!!" came the shouts of his teammates.

"What a shot!" Greg yelled.

"Awesome," added Cole.

"Way to keep your composure and your head in the game," said Kyle who was still standing close by. He gave Morgan a slap on the back. Morgan grinned sheepishly.

"Luck," he said, but Kyle would have none of it.

"Not by a long shot," he said. "That took some skill and composure. Nice shootin'."

The boys continued their round, helping each other line up shots, read the greens, look for lost balls, then offer advice and encouragement, and remind each other of the rules. At the end of nine holes, they headed for the clubhouse to get a soda and sit outside where they could watch other golfers drive off the first tee.

"That was a lot of fun," Morgan said once they all had a seat. "I'm glad I joined the team. I don't know the rules very well though as you can see."

"That comes with just playing and reading the rule book," Greg said. "Sometimes the application doesn't become clear until you are actually in the situation. You have a really natural swing," he added.

"Thanks," Morgan said a bit embarrassed, "but you noticed that every once in a while I really sliced it."

"You just blocked yourself," Cole said. "Didn't allow your hands to come through and your wrists to release."

Morgan nodded. "Glad you were there to remind me," he said.

The conversation continued covering all the aspects of golf, then on to the baseball season and which pro teams would end up in the World Series even though that was seven months away.

"Well, it's been fun, guys," Kyle said, "but I got to get going. My grandparents are coming next week and Mom has a list of chores for me to do this weekend. I want to get a couple done tonight so I have *some* Saturday to myself. Cole, Greg, see you guys at church on Sunday."

"Yup," they both answered. "See you there."

After Kyle left, Greg turned toward Morgan.

"Do you go to church anywhere, Morgan?" he asked.

"No, not really. I've been a couple of times," he answered.

"Are you a Christian?" Cole asked.

"Yeah. I am," he answered.

Greg looked puzzled.

"Then why don't you go to church?" he asked.

"Why do I need to?" he countered. "I know what I believe. I don't have to go to church to prove anything."

Greg looked puzzled. Both he and Cole were quiet for a minute. Finally, Greg spoke up.

"You're not trying to prove anything," he said, "but you fellowship with other Christians for the very same reason you play golf with your teammates."

Now it was Morgan's turn to look-puzzled.

"What?" he asked. "What does golf have to do with it?"

Greg shook his head. "Nothing directly" he said, "but think about it. Golf is a sport that a person can play all by him- or herself. It's just you against the course, right?"

"Right," Morgan agreed.

"But if you played golf *only* by yourself, what would you miss out on? Think about today. What would have been different had you played this round today all by yourself?"

Morgan thought about it for a moment.

"I wouldn't have learned the rules for dropping out of a hazard, for one," he said.

Greg nodded. "And?" he asked.

"I wouldn't have had someone there to remind me not to block my shots, or encourage me, or help me line up my putts, or…" The analogy was beginning to dawn on him.

"You getting the picture now?" Greg asked.

"I think so," Morgan said.

"You're right. You don't have to go to church to prove anything," Greg said, "and going to church doesn't save you. But just like your golf buddies on the course, other Christians give you that same support and encouragement and accountability and those reminders that make taking on the world a bit easier. Sure you can go it alone though no Christian is ever alone – but sometimes the world seems a lot more overwhelming when you don't have your Christian buddies around you.

"Also," Cole added, "just like the entire playing experience is better in golf when you are with your teammates, so is the whole Christian experience better when shared with other Christians, and that's not limited to church. Your relationship with Christ can grow even here on the golf course.

Morgan nodded his head in agreement and thought about

his round. What had started on the first hole, according to Mark Twain, as a "good walk spoiled," had ended up being one of the best walks he had ever had.

A Rock and a Hard Place

WHAP!

The pine branch swung back and smacked Sarah right in the face.

"Ouch!" she yelped.

From two strides ahead Craig turned around to see what was wrong.

"Uh, sorry," he said when he saw her angrily pushing the branch out of her face. "I didn't know it would whip back like that."

"Well, what did you think it would do?" Sarah muttered under her breath. "Man, I knew I shouldn't have come."

"You don't like hiking?" Craig asked, trying to switch the focus.

"I don't like scarring my face, ruining my nails, getting my feet wet in freezing water, slipping down muddy embankments…" she paused. "No, I guess you could say I don't like hiking very much," she said sarcastically.

Craig felt his face grow red.

"Don't you at least like being outdoors?" he asked. "It's so beautiful." He let his own gaze sweep up and down the trail covered with the bright green of spring. "And so quiet."

"Quiet?" Sarah asked in disbelief. "You've got to be kidding. I haven't been able to hear myself think for the last half hour because of that stupid rushing river."

"Hey! What's the hold up?" someone yelled from behind.

"Guess we'd better get moving," Craig said. "People are anxious."

"Yeah, OK," Sarah agreed, "but watch the branches."

Craig nodded meekly and headed on. Sarah let him get a healthy head start before she started after him. No need pressing her luck.

She felt her legs groan as they started uphill again.

I thought this was supposed to be an easy hike, she thought. *That's the only reason I even agreed to come on this thing.*

This *thing* she was referring to was the youth department's hike to Porter Creek Falls. Their youth minister, Phil Swenson, said it would provide an object lesson for last week's lesson and lead into this week's.

The only objects I'm learning anything about are these stupid branches. Stay clear.

The roar of the creek – river to Sarah – was almost deafening now, but still she could hear loud whoops of approval up ahead.

Could this possibly be the end of the hike? she thought and almost felt a tingle of contentment.

But when she cleared the next rise and went around a small bend, she saw what all the hollering was about. Below her, one at a time, the group was crossing the raging river on a narrow log. Her heart froze.

No way, she thought. *Never!*

"Hey! Keep moving! What's holding you up?"

Despite her fears Sarah knew she at least had to go down to the river, if only to let people pass her. She made her way down carefully and then looked at the scene before her. To her surprise there were actually two logs. One to step across on, or slide sideways on, and the other, about two feet higher, to hold onto. From this angle it didn't look too bad at all. She fell into line and took her turn.

Midway out she looked down, and was surprised to see the force and power of the water pulsing beneath her. Squeezed between the rocks, its force almost doubled as it shot downstream.

"Hey! Keep moving!"

"Just hold your horses," she muttered again, and moved on.

Once across she headed up the embankment that the others had taken and found the first of the group waiting in a small clearing just above the liquid turmoil below.

"Over here," Phil yelled and waved her and those behind her over. In a matter of minutes, Mrs. Brady who had volunteered to shore up the rear, straggled in with the rest of them.

"We're about half way to our destination," he explained, "and I wanted to take this opportunity to make a point."

He glanced down the embankment toward the rushing water.

"What do you notice about that water?" he asked.

"It's cold!" someone yelled.

"It's fast!" came another.

"It could wash you right downstream if you're not careful," Sarah said half under her breath.

The youth minister heard her and smiled.

"Perfect," he said. "Now why does it have so much power?"

"Cause there's a lot of water," came one cry.

"Wrong!" he answered. "Well, partially right."

"Because all that water has to go in that little space between those rocks," Sarah answered. "Did you guys see how it just shot out of there?" She was getting into it.

Phil's smile grew bigger.

"Yes!" he said. "Object lesson number one. The rocks in the stream or riverbed are the very things that provide the setting for the water's power. Now how does this fit in with last week's lesson?"

Silence. Except for the deafening roar of the water.

"You mean about the Holy Spirit and Pentecost?" Jason asked. Phil nodded.

"Well, the Holy Spirit showed His power through the disciples," Craig volunteered.

"Yes, but why was it so powerful?"

Sarah suddenly felt an awareness of what he was driving at.

"Because there were so many rocks," she yelled. The others all turned to stare.

"Peter?" someone asked. Sarah shook her head.

"No, rocks… problems… tribulations," she said. "Don't you see. The disciples and all of Christ's followers were what you might say caught between a rock and a hard place. Their Lord was gone. They were few in number, in a huge city, and surrounded by thousands of people who spoke tons of different languages."

"So," Craig picked up. "The power of the Holy Spirit was focused and funneled."

"Now, how is this applicable to you today?" their youth minister asked.

From the back, "Consider it pure joy, my brothers, whenever you face trials of many kinds…"

The group laughed but caught the meaning.

"True," Phil agreed. "Though the Holy Spirit can work thorough us in any situation, often it is when we are in the tightest and most uncomfortable spots that we see His power the most."

He stood up.

"Let's move on," he said. "I have one more thing to show you."

Sarah rose with the others, forgetting all her earlier discomfort and anxious to see what was next.

The path rose up into the mountain ever higher, and the river returned to being a stream and then finally a small brook. Phil had them sit again.

"This is as far as we go," he said, "but I do wish I could take you to the source of the river."

"It doesn't matter," Kevin popped up. "It wouldn't be too impressive anyway. Just a trickle of water."

Phil's face lit up with that smile that always betrayed his inner thoughts. It was the smile that said, *You just hit on an important spiritual truth and you haven't realized it yet.*

Sarah saw it and the impact of the little, unimpressive sliver of water hit her with greater force than the switch of that branch that had left a stripe on her face. As the little creek accumulated more water and made its way downstream; as it bobbled over pebbles and pushed itself around rocks in its way; as it grew in size, it grew in power. *Was she?* she wondered. *"Was she adding spiritual water for her journey so that as she hit the pebbles and rocks in her life, the power of the Holy Spirit was evident?"*

"Need I say more?" asked Phil.

Point of View

"**B**URNEY!" I yelled at the top of my lungs. "Get over here!"

From around the corner of the house, Burney came at a sprint, but when she saw me standing next to Mom's flower bed with my hands on my hips and my feet spread in my most authoritarian stance, she stopped dead in her tracks.

"Burney! Come here!"

She looked up at me warily; her head hung low in dejection. She inched her way toward me ever so slowly. Half way she stopped. She knew what she had done, and she knew what was in store.

"Burney! Get over here!"

She slid closer. When she finally reached my feet, she rolled over, revealing her stomach in a sign of submission. It didn't work. I rolled her over and scolded her.

Then I grabbed her by the collar, pulled her to the offending hole, and stuck her face in it.

"No!" I yelled. "Bad dog!"

I didn't know if it was sinking in, or if I was destroying her vulnerable doggie ego. After all, I hadn't read one book on doggie parenting, but somehow getting upset and letting her know about it seemed the right thing to do. It seemed to be working. She hung her head in appropriate contrition and looked up at me with those apologetic brown cocker eyes. I took her head in my hands again and stared straight into those baby browns.

"Bad dog," I repeated, then stood up and walked away. She followed contritely right at my heels so that I almost tripped trying to go through the patio door. She hugged close to me trying to slip in. "No," I said. "You stay outside. You've been a bad dog." And I closed the screen door on her.

She watched me disappear into the family room. Once out of sight I went out the other door and back into the kitchen where she couldn't see me watching her. She sat at the door a few minutes waiting and hoping that I or somebody might return and let her in. When no one did, she went over to the flowerbed, sniffed at the hole she had made, and then returned to the patio door and lay down to wait.

By this time I wasn't mad any more. After all, she was so cute; I just couldn't stay mad too long. I came out of hiding and slid open the door.

"Come on in," I said resignedly. "I hope you've learned your lesson."

She trotted in and stood next to me.

"Now I don't want any more of this digging, do you understand?" I asked, still keeping a stern tone in my voice. She looked up at me innocently. "OK. You can stay inside."

I turned to go to my room and Burney followed closely, so closely I almost tripped over her again.

"Burney!" I yelled. "Move out of the way!"

But she wouldn't. She stayed right next to me. I smiled in spite of myself, sat down in the middle of the hallway, and pulled her into my lap.

"All right, all right," I said, rubbing her head between my hands the way she liked. "I'm not mad at you anymore. I love you," and gave her a kiss on the nose. She licked mine as I laughed and hugged her. "But you can't dig in Mom's flower bed. OK?"

She smiled that doggie smile of hers, and that hind end wiggled with a vengeance. I laughed again.

"Go on now," I said pushing her away. "Go play. Leave me alone."

She jumped off my lap and sped down the hall, losing her footing on the wood entryway and sliding into the wall. I cracked up. She regained her composure, took off again, and in a minute she was back squeaking her obnoxious piece of rubber celery, ready to play. I couldn't believe it. It was as if she had never been in trouble, and I had never punished her. As far as she was concerned, it was time to play.

I grabbed for the celery, and she held on tight, letting out a playful growl.

"Well, how am I supposed to play with you if you won't give it to me?" I asked. She relinquished her hold and sat, her mouth back in that doggie smile, her bobbed tail wiggling, just waiting in anticipation for my throw. I shook my head in disbelief and let it fly. She was gone in a flash. I heard the squeaking and knew she was on her way back. She came back in the room, but instead of bringing it to me, she went to her pillow and lay down. That was enough for her. She knew she had been forgiven, restored to her rightful position. Kind of like Baby on *Dinosaurs*: "I'm the baby, gotta love me."

I lay down on my bed and looked at her over there primping herself. I've learned a lot from Burney. What it means to be loyal. What it means to accept forgiveness, to actually crave it.

I pursed my lips. I've always reacted in the complete opposite. Like two weeks ago when I was caught in the web of gossip. It had seemed fun at the time, being with the "in" group, getting to hear all the juicy gossip, and then being entrusted to pass it on to just the right people. Quite an ego trip.

That was until I realized that none of it was true, that it really hurt Diane, the victim, and that she along with most of the school knew that I was a part of the gossipers. Had I asked for forgiveness either from Diane or God? Had I groveled and hugged their sides until they forgave me? Far from it. I kept as far away from both of them as I could. I avoided Diane like the plague because I was so embarrassed. I avoided God too. I felt so unworthy that I refused to open my Bible because I might taint it.

Yesterday, my mom finally dragged a confession out of me and then told me to get in the car and go over to Diane's to apologize. Mom's so subtle.

Well, I did, and it wasn't easy. I didn't look Diane in the face while I mumbled out my apologies and asked for her forgiveness. I think I heard her say she forgave me, but I wasn't really listening. I figured there was no way she would ever really like me again, so I vowed I was still going to avoid her.

When I returned home, Mom asked how it went, and I shrugged a very despondent, "I don't know." She sent me to my room to ask God's forgiveness.

In a way this was both easier and harder. Easier in that I could apologize and not see anyone in front of me, but harder because I knew my whole Christian testimony was shot. The entire school knew I was one of the gossip mongers, so my credibility was nil.

I got on my knees, buried my head in my bedspread, and muffled out my second apology to ask God for forgiveness. Even though the Bible says He forgives and forgets instantaneously, I doubted His sincerity as much as I did Diane's. He was through with me I was sure. He couldn't use such a sinner.

I lay down on my bed and stared at the ceiling, not thinking of anything in particular when I heard a knock on the door.

"Mind if I come in?" Mom asked. I waved her in, and she sat on the edge of the bed.

"Peter or Paul?" she asked. I looked at her like she'd lost it.

"What are you talking about?" I asked.

"Which one do you feel like right now?" she asked.

"Neither," I answered vehemently. "They were *good* Christians. I feel more like Judas."

"Wrong answer and wrong attitude," she replied.

"What do you mean?"

"I mean both of them made mistakes and could have thought God couldn't use them," she answered. "Peter publicly denied Christ three times, and Paul publicly persecuted Christians."

"Yeah, but God turned them into great people," I retaliated.

"Wrong answer and wrong attitude again," Mom said. "You're not doing too well on this quiz show I'm afraid."

"What do you mean wrong answer and wrong attitude?"

"God was only able to make them into great people because they accepted God's forgiveness and made themselves available to Him again. You're lying here saying it's impossible. That you're through. Now what kind of attitude is that?"

She walked out, and I was left to think about what she

had said. No flashes of revelation, no sudden understanding. Nothing. That is until today. And who taught me?

Burney! No wonder dogs are considered man's best friend. They teach us the most valuable lessons.

70 times 7

If that little runt doesn't stay out of my stuff I'm going to –" Mark stopped short, not exactly sure what he would do but still mad enough to do it. "Joey!" he yelled. "Joey, get in here!"

Within seconds an eight-year-old with a shock of tousled brown hair and grass-stained jeans appeared ruefully in the doorway. Mark turned on him with a vengeance.

"Have you been listening to my tapes?" he yelled, holding out one of the empty cases.

Joey swallowed hard and his eyes widened. Finally he managed a weak nod, his eyes never leaving Mark's face.

"Well, where is it?" It's not in the case."

Joey seemed to turn gray. Desperately he searched Mark's room for the tape, finally finding it lodged between the speaker and the bed. He handed it back to Mark.

"I'm sorry, Mark," he said. "I won't use it again."

"You bet you won't," Mark agreed. "Now go on."

Later at dinner Joey ate in silence, eyeing Mark shyly. Mark ignored him but no one else seemed to notice. Karissa, their thirteen-year-old sister, was talking incessantly as usual.

Finally, Mr. McAlister broke in. "Mark, have you seen my electrician's tool kit?" he asked.

"Oh, it's in my room," Mark answered.

Mr. McAlister looked surprised. "What's it doing in there?"

"I was doing a little work on my stereo last night and forgot to put it back. Sorry." Then with concern he added, "Did you need it?"

"I wouldn't be asking if I didn't," his father replied. He laid down his fork. "Mark, I don't mind you using my tools. Just remember to put them back, all right?"

"Sure, Dad. Sorry. I'll get it after dinner." Mark paused a moment and then continued, changing the subject. "Can you let me use the car Saturday? Some of the guys are getting together with the coach around nine for some extra practice. Then we're going over to watch the double-A game in Marion."

Mark's license was barely a week old. He saw doubt in his father's face so he hastened to explain. "I'd ride with the other guys, but it's a double header, and I don't want to stay for the night game."

The explanation seemed to help. "I guess so," Mr. McAlister said. "But you have to promise me two things."

Mark was ecstatic. "Anything," he promised.

"First, you'll drive carefully –"

"I will," he said, resentful of being treated like a child.

"And second, that you'll pick up some important documents for me at the accountant's office on the way to Marion. They're only open until one on Saturday and I need to complete some work Saturday night. Deal?"

"Deal!" Mark answered enthusiastically.

• • •

Mark didn't wake up till after eight Saturday and had to hustle to be out at the field by nine. He ate a quick breakfast, grabbed his gear and the car keys, and yelled goodbye.

"Don't forget the accountant," his dad reminded him.

"I won't," he said and was out the door.

In the dugout he reached in his bag for his glove. He stopped short. He looked again.

"That little brat!" he fumed. "Can't he leave my stuff alone?"

"What's wrong?" the second baseman, Gary, asked.

Mark shook his head and his breath came in short hard spurts. "My little brother took my glove out," he said between clenched teeth. "And obviously he didn't put it back."

Are you sure you just didn't forget it?" Gary asked.

Mark gave him a hard look and Gary threw up his hands in surrender. "OK. OK. But don't get so steamed. Coach has a few extra."

"Yeah, right," Mark mumbled and grabbed his bat. As he had expected, practice went terribly. Every time he made an error he would stare at the borrowed glove in disgust. When practice was over, he threw his stuff in the car and joined the caravan to Marion. The visiting team won the double-A game, and by the time Mark reached home, he was in a foul mood.

He slammed the door behind him. "Where is he?" he screamed as he stomped through the house.

Mark went to his room, and there was his glove lying innocently on his bed. He grabbed it and went back to the family room where his parents were sitting.

"That little thief has gone too far this time!" he blurted, his face red with fury. "Do you know what he did?"

Mr. McAlister folded his paper slowly and laid it next to his chair. "Yes, we know what he did," he said with control in his voice. "Joey told us."

Mark shook the glove. "I don't ever want him near my stuff, my room, or me for that matter, ever!"

His father clenched his jaw and raised his eyebrows. "Well, then. How about if you stay away from my tools, the car, and from me?"

Mark's mouth dropped open. "But, Dad –"

"You didn't stop at the accountant's," his father interrupted. "They called me."

The blood drained from Mark's face.

"Oh, Dad, I'm sorry," he stammered. "I was just so mad I forgot."

"So did your brother."

Mark swallowed hard.

"And what about my tools last week?"

Mark felt sick. "I – I said I was sorry, and I put them back."

"And Joey found your tape." He stared long and hard at Mark. "You'd like me to forgive you, assume you've learned your lesson, and give you a second chance. But it seems to me you're asking for more than you're willing to give."

Mark looked uncomfortably at the offending glove. A slight movement caught his eye and he glanced up in time to see the tousled brown hair pull back out of the doorway.

"Joey," he said quietly. The small boy stepped through the door, poking some imaginary mark on the floor with the toe of his sneaker. He didn't look up.

"I'm sorry, Joey," Mark said quietly. "Will you forgive me?"

Joey looked up in surprise, first at Mark, and then at his father. He nodded quickly. "I'm sorry too, Mark," he said, and then stood there as if he were wondering what to do.

"There's still a little light left," Mark began. "You want

to throw a few? You can use my glove."

Joey's face lit up. "Sure!"

"Grab the ball and my old glove out of my room and I'll meet you out back."

Joey obediently hustled off to get the gear. Mark reached into his pocket and handed the car keys back to his father. "I feel terrible about forgetting your papers, Dad. How will you get your work done?"

"I won't get it done," Mr. McAlister answered. "I suppose I'll ask for an extension on my deadline and work late at the office on Monday. For now, though, I have some unexpected free time. How about I join you guys in the back yard?"

The Cost

"Gwen, you have got to come shopping with us tomorrow. It is the first day of the big summer sale."

Gwen smiled. There was nothing she loved more than a sale.

"Sounds great. Where and when do you want to meet?"

Brooke and Alyssa looked at each other, raised their eyebrows, shrugged shoulders, pursed lips, but never said a word, yet their telepathy was at work.

"Nine o'clock in front of The Buckle," Brooke announced and Alyssa nodded her head vigorously.

Gwen stared at them in amazement.

"Nine?" The stores don't open until eleven."

"But we need to be at the doors when they do," stated Brooke.

"And we need to be first," exclaimed Alyssa, "or all the good stuff will be gone."

Unfortunately, I won't be able to meet up with you until

about 12:30," Gwen stated.

"But all the good bargains will be gone by then," Alyssa repeated and Brooke nodded vigorously.

Now it was Gwen's turn to shrug her shoulders.

"That's just the chance I will have to take," she said. "Church isn't over until 10:30 and then we always have a Sunday brunch as a family with each of us making something. I think I am on hash brown duty this week," she added smiling.

The look of incredulity on the other two girls' faces grew.

"You actually eat breakfast as a family?" Brooke asked.

"You can't miss church this once for something important like this?" Alyssa added. "The sale only comes once a year and church is every week. Plus, wearing the newest trends will make you popular."

Gwen listened to her friends' arguments. She had heard them many times before and had also witnessed the aftermath, even experiencing it herself on a couple of occasions.

It was the way of the world with Satan as the master deceiver. Over and over again, he would throw out enticing opportunities to tempt God's people from putting Him first. And, of course, each event happened "only once a year" while church was every week. Once there was the NFL playoffs scheduled for 10 a.m. Sure they came every year, and true you could tape it and view it later, but this might be the *only* time the local team made it, and since so many people would be talking about it, you were bound to hear the results before you had a chance to watch it, so how could you miss it, flew the arguments.

If it wasn't the playoffs, it was always something else. There was always a special sale that would provide one with the most stunning outfit or a discounted computer or tablet. There was always that gossip to pass along to show you were one of those "in the know." Or looking at just a couple of answers isn't so bad. Everyone does it and those extra points could get you that A which might get you a bit closer to that college you wanted.

But the result was undoubtedly the same: once the score was recorded the euphoria of winning evaporated within a couple of days if not immediately. And if the team had lost, well, it might have been better not to have witnessed it.

The outfit was indeed stunning, but after it was worn – even once – it was no longer unique and the popularity purchasing power was gone. Someone else always knew a bit more gossip and often the cheating scheme unraveled.

Gwen remembered her mother relenting once, when Gwen threw what could only be termed a borderline tantrum about not being allowed to *anything* fun because of church. She had then been allowed to go on a shopping excursion with her friends and had returned home ecstatic with her purchases and proudly showed them off to her family, who all agreed that they were indeed very nice and that she looked stunning in them, but then that was that.

The dinner conversation had turned to the morning's sermon and God's ability and desire to provide all our needs, and Gwen had felt left out. Not so much because she had missed the sermon since she knew this attribute of God, but because she hadn't experienced the fellowship and community of her brothers and sisters in Christ. Whereas the feeling from her shopping spree only lasted as long as the glory of her clothes did, the satisfaction and sense of oneness from fellowshipping with other believers had no expiration date. Though she might forget about the message as her daily routine seeped back in, invariably it would return to sustain her through tough times. While clothes, victories, technology, and personal achievements lost their lustre over the years and had to be replaced or built upon, God's words and promises never diminished.

Some of her friends had sacrificed even more in their search for love and significance by pushing God's safety boundaries in order to prove their love of feel secure or worthwhile, only to encounter disappointment and hurt later on. The world's values and rewards were transitory while God's were eternal.

A slight smile escaped Gwen's lips. She could live without a few more bargains this year, even if it did mean a step down on the high school popularity ladder.

"Well?" Brooke asked.

Gwen shook her head.

"Sorry to disappoint you," she answered. "but I am going to have to say no. I have a feeling this shopping spree will cost me more than I am willing to pay."

Miguel
Part 1 of 3

The bell rang and Miguel packed up his books and stood to leave, but before he could even get to his feet, students rushed past him and out the door, inadvertently pushing him back into his seat. He sat and waited until the others had left and then stood again.

"You doing alright?"

Miguel looked toward the front of the class to where Mr. Springhorn was standing, smiling sympathetically at him. Miguel nodded.

"It will take a bit of time to get used to everything," Mr. Springhorn said. Miguel nodded again, picked up his books and walked out of the classroom.

Students were still streaming past him, down the hall and toward the quad where the cafeteria was located. Miguel hung back and watched as they swarmed around him, and he felt himself jostled and pushed again as they hurried by. A minute later, however, he found the hallway deserted and himself alone.

Slowly he moved past classrooms and toward the cafeteria. Lunchtime. As he exited the door and neared the quad, he could hear laughter floating from every angle as were foul language and taunts. Miguel kept walking, trying not to stick out but feeling very much out of place even though no one paid him any attention.

He felt his stomach rumble. It had been five hours since breakfast. He licked his lips. His mother had signed him up for the free lunch program, so he knew food was waiting for him. He opened the cafeteria door and stared, then felt himself go cold. He stepped back outside, surveyed the quad, got his bearings, and headed toward the gym. He could spend the lunch hour behind the gym and no one would see him.

Miguel rounded the corner. Empty. He let out a sigh of relief and sat down on the blacktop basketball court and leaned against the gym wall and closed his eyes.

"Father," he prayed. "I'm hurting. I am so lonely."

He wasn't lying. His entire insides ached, and he felt wave after wave of loneliness sweep over him. It was March and this year his world had been turned inside out *and* thrown for a loop, because of California's drought.

Miguel's parents were migrant workers and had been ever since he was born. Each year they would start in the Imperial Valley and work their way up the state, working the asparagus and lettuce fields in the south, the peach and almond orchards in the San Joaquin and Sacramento Valleys until they finished with the olives and walnuts in Northern California. Like clockwork they would move from town to town but in the past it had always been the same towns, and all small towns: El Centro, Selma, Williams, Corning. Same town, same teachers, same friends. Though they moved regularly, Miguel could predict within two days when he would be enrolling in his next school. Those towns knew about migrant workers, their kids, and their education.

But this year was different. The water wasn't there so the crops weren't there or at least not enough crops to sustain all the workers, so his parents had had to augment their income by coming into Sacramento and looking for some other work while they waited for the next crops to come in, and the city had big schools with lots of students. Miguel, his head still bowed, continued to pray.

"I don't know if I can do this, Lord," he cried silently. "I don't have the strength to push myself again. To make new friends. Give me your strength, Lord. Give me your strength."

He said a silent "amen," gave a heavy sigh, and rested his chin on his arms that were resting on his knees. He squinted a bit, tilted his head, and looked again.

What is that? he thought and pushed himself to his feet and walked across the blacktop toward a clump of weeds near the fence. He pushed the weeds aside and saw what had caught his attention. A basketball!

"Yeah!" Miguel exclaimed, the first smile of the day crossing his lips. "Oh, yeah!" he said again, grabbing it and giving it a trial bounce. Full. Not flat. Good deal.

He bounced it again, from one hand to the other and then took a tentative dribble out to the court. He loved basketball. At five foot seven he knew he wasn't going to be an NBA player, but he had some moves. In a normal year, he would be in Selma during the basketball season and had played for one of their teams. This year they had moved right in the middle of January, cutting his season short.

He felt a brief pang of regret, but that immediately dissipated as he feinted to his left and drove the basket for an easy layup.

"Who da man?" he yelled.

"You da man!" he answered.

For the next fifteen minutes he dribbled around imaginary defenders, took twenty-foot jumpers, and toed the free throw line to drain last second free throws to win the game. He had forgotten all about being hungry.

Suddenly, he heard the bell ring right as he was releasing his half-court game winning Hail Mary. The sound startled him and the shot jarred off the front of the rim.

Miguel felt himself come back to earth and the gloom that had plagued him all day threatened to settle back over him, but he shook it off.

"I'm okay, Lord," he said. "Thank you. Thank you for the basketball."

He glanced around the outdoor courts, looking for a safer place to stow the ball until tomorrow. He spotted some bushes at the far end of the court and pushed the ball to the back and then walked out to mid-court to take a look. Nothing. The ball was securely hidden. He smiled wryly. He was feeling better now. Jesus was indeed his friend, and now he had a second friend –a basketball. He let out a soft sigh. He knew that in time he would have more – in time.

The Fantastic Five

Part 2 of 3

"Peter, John, Paul, Sam, and David."

David raised one finger for each of his friends and then his thumb for himself until his palm was wide open, fingers spread apart.

"Alone, vulnerable and unprotected," he said, "but together with Christ as our center (and here he placed a small cross in the center of his palm and slowly closed his fingers into a fist) we are strong."

As he had been speaking, his four friends had been mirroring all he had been doing with their own hands, and when all five had a closed fist, those fists met in the middle of the circle for a group fist bump.

"Peter, it's your turn," David said, and Peter nodded and the five friends bowed their heads.

"Lord Jesus," he began, "thank you for being our Lord and protector. May we hold each other up in prayer and deed, and may we be a light to our dark world. Amen."

"Amen," echoed the other four and the heads came up,

the fists retracted, and the crosses went into their pants' pockets as a constant reminder of who they represented.

Almost to the second, a bell rang, signaling classes would be starting in five minutes.

"And we're off!" shouted David, and the five of them dispersed into five different directions.

The five friends had been following a similar routine since they had met in the seventh grade, the second day at Hamilton Middle School. They had come from five different grammar schools and represented five different ethnic groups: John was Vietnamese; Paul, African-American; Sam, Native American of the California Modoc tribe; David was Jewish; and Peter was the token Heinz 57. The only thing the five had in common was that they were all small, which is how they were thrown together. The second day of school was the first day of dressing out for PE and in all his wisdom, the PE teacher had the kids divide themselves into teams of five for the first unit— basketball. By default the five found themselves together on a team. By everyone else's design they found themselves in last place by the end of the unit. None of them were any good at basketball, and even if they had been, none of them would have been able to shoot over the outstretched hands of their classmates.

However, what had turned out to be a disaster in PE turned out to be a stroke of good fortune everywhere else – at least that is what three of the boys had thought. David and John knew otherwise, because David was a Messianic Jew and John a Vietnamese Christian, and both had heard enough family stories of God's deliverance to know that good fortune was the world's way of sidestepping God's involvement.

It hadn't taken David or John long to learn that the other was a Christian and the two started to compare notes. Both had feared leaving their small grammar schools for the fifteen hundred plus middle school, and both had prayed that God would take care of them, for Hamilton Middle School had a reputation for being rough. On day two, God had started answering that prayer and working on the five young boys who would become close friends and impact a middle school and later a high school.

After that first, discouraging day in PE, the boys made a vow – "stay together, play together." And so the ritual began. No one's sure exactly who came up with the idea or if it just kind of morphed, but each morning they would meet in front of the school, a different boy reciting the names and leading the hand movements. The reminder of their friendship gave them the emotional strength for the day but also came in handy in some very tangible struggles as well—in the hallways and on the playing fields. Their small stature made them a sure target for those who thought they would back down. But they hadn't, and only once had they actually had to fight.

Most of their success came, ironically, on the basketball court. After that initial experience in PE, Paul, who walked to school, convinced his dad to buy him a basketball, and he would bring it to school, and every day, religiously at lunch and then after school whenever they could, the boys practiced. They created plays that emphasized speed and deception and worked on defenses that kept the bigger boys from ever getting near the basket. By the end of the basketball unit that first year, though they had finished last, they had won a game and earned both respect and a name – the Fantastic Five.

Within two years, after David and John had shared their faith in Christ with their new friends, the other three had accepted Christ, and the group added a third part to their slogan –"pray together" – and a third part to their ritual – the cross in the middle of their palm and then in the pocket. Basketball had become their second salvation so all five read everything they could, and it was Peter, whose father was a UCLA alumnus who had heard how the legendary UCLA coach John Wooden would always keep a cross in his pocket to remind him of who was really in control and who he was responsible to.

The boys continued their basketball success as they graduated from middle school to high school, and it didn't hurt that they grew as well – well, Paul, Peter, and Sam and David grew. John topped out at five-six and would forever be a guard. Their faith and commitment to Christ grew as well, and the morning fist pumps that first began as an emotional boost before a fearful and challenging day, had now become a commitment to seeking out new challenges for Christ.

Now as juniors, they made it a point, either individually or as a group, to enter into someone else's world each day and touch that person in some way: a smile, a coke, a ride home, some help on a chemistry problem. Little did they know that someone was about to enter into theirs as well.

Star of David

Part 3 of 3

"Do you see him?"

"No. Do you?"

"Nope. Maybe he doesn't have lunch now."

"He has lunch now because I have lunch now, and we both have chemistry next. He has to have lunch now."

David, John, Sam, Peter, and Paul – aka the Fantastic Five – gave the cafeteria another once over, trying to see if they could find the new boy.

"What did you say his name was?" Sam asked.

"Miguel," replied John.

"That helps," Paul said. "At least I kind of know what I am looking for. I'm guessing he's brown, just not as brown as me."

"That would be right," David acknowledged, "since you are chocolate."

"Dark chocolate," Paul corrected, "and lovin' every minute of it."

"Anyway," Peter interjected, "it doesn't look like he's

here. He must have found someone to eat with, so why don't we get in line. I'm starving!"

Sam was the only one who hadn't said anything, and as the others headed toward the line, he hung back. The others stopped.

"What's the problem?" David asked.

Sam shook his head. "He's hiding," he said. "Lunch is the absolute worst time to be new and know no one. No, he's somewhere… just not here."

"Maybe he's already made a friend," John said. "After all, this is his second day here."

Silence fell over the group as a new thought dawned.

"Hadn't thought about that," Peter said.

"Neither did I," said David.

"Hmmm," grunted Sam.

"What?" asked John. "That he made a friend?"

"No," said Paul, "that he might *need* a friend. We were just thinking about inviting him to have lunch with us. We weren't really thinking past that. Are you guys thinking what I'm thinking?"

The others nodded… except John who was still in the dark.

"What?" he asked again.

Peter looked at him. "What if he wants to be *our* friend," he asked.

"So?" said John.

"So we're the Fantastic Five," stated Paul, raising his

hand, palm facing out, and as he named each friend, closing it into a fist. " David, John, Peter, Sam, and Paul. Five… not six. How do you do six?"

John finally got the picture. "Oh. Hadn't thought about that."

The boys fell silent again. Peter's stomach rumbled, but he didn't feel like eating anymore. This was a tough one. They prided themselves being Godly teenagers: being God's hands and feet and helping others, holding each other accountable, encouraging each other. But they had never had to change *who* they were. They were and would always be the Fantastic Five… at least they had thought they would.

"So what do we do?" asked John. "Forget about him?"

"Maybe this is God's way of telling us not to worry about him," Peter suggested. "After all, God brought the five of us together in the first place, right? In seventh grade no less. And he has been using us – the five of us – to do pretty good things, wouldn't you agree? So maybe us not being able to find this new guy is God's way of saying he wants it to stay just the five of us."

The other four looked at him. Peter's rationale sounded great, especially because it was what they all wanted to hear, but in their hearts they didn't believe it.

Paul took a deep breath and shook his head.

"I know it would be tough change," he said, "but I really can't believe we're debating this. Kind of sad. This guy may not even *want* to be our friend. That's not what God put on our heart. All God has said was find him and invite him to have lunch with us, and here we are worried about protecting our little group." He paused just briefly before adding the finishing touch – "our clique."

John started to protest, but Paul's raised eyebrow stopped him. He knew Paul was right. They all knew Paul was right. They were just embarrassed to admit it.

"Six could work," Sam said.

"Yeah," agreed Peter. "I like nice even figures. Yeah. Six is good."

"A Star of David," said David.

"Say what?" John asked. "Why do you have a star named after you?"

"It's not named after me," David retorted. "The Star of David is a symbol of the Jewish people. It has six points instead of five," David explained. "It's made up of two interlocking triangles."

The others continued to stare.

"Why?" Sam finally asked.

David shrugged. "Number of different ideas, but the most common is each point represents a direction: north, south, east, west, up, down and God governs all. He is at the center.

More silence.

"I like it," Paul said.

"Me too," John added.

"Plus we don't have a light brown guy to balance out dark chocolate here," Sam added, shooting Paul a grin.

"Good point," said David seriously, not realizing Sam had been joking.

"Let's go find this guy," Peter suggested and the five set off.

They soon determined he was nowhere in the cafeteria, so headed out to the quad, then across it and toward the gym. As they approached the gym corner, they could hear the faint sound of a ball bouncing, followed by the soft swish of a net. The five looked at each other and grinned.

They rounded the corner and there he was – all five-feet-seven inches of him. They watched as he took the ball, dribbled deftly to his left, feinted right throwing off his imaginary opponent and then released a twenty foot jumper that hit nothing but net.

The five applauded.

"Nice shot!" shouted Sam.

The boy turned, surprised to see someone there. The five walked toward him.

"Nice ball handling," David said.

"Great shooting," added Peter.

The guy smiled slightly.

"Thanks," he said.

"I'm Paul," Paul began and the others introduced themselves as well.

"Miguel," the boy replied.

"Mind if we join you?" John said. "We could do a little three on three."

Miguel's smile widened.

"That'd be great," he said.

The five looked at each other and grinned as well. *Three on three. Something they had never been able to do before. Perhaps this would work into two interlocking triangles of three. Perhaps this was going to be six points with God in the center representing God's sovereignty over the whole universe rather than His guidance over five friends. Perhaps... the boys could speculate all they wanted but for right now, it was a game of three on three with a new kid who could shoot the pants off any of them.*

Chipping Away

Adam took a step back from the block of soapstone, looked it over, and began to smile. He could see the figure begin to emerge and come to life.

"So this is what Michelangelo meant when he said, 'I saw the angel in the marble and carved until I set him free,'" Adam murmured. "Well, I see a bear, and he is on his way to roaming the world."

Adam surveyed the sculpture and then picked up a finer chisel and started to work again. *I can also understand when he said "It is well with me only when I have a chisel in my hand,"* he thought. *I love sculpting.*

Adam loved art – period. End of story. This was his fourth year, and this year he had been introduced to sculpture. Though he had enjoyed painting and drawing and even ceramics, not until he started sculpting did he feel that he had found his calling. He felt just like Michelangelo did when he said, "Every block of stone has a statue inside it and it is the task of the sculptor to discover it." That's exactly what Adam wanted to do – discover and release those hidden forms. He chipped away another piece of soapstone. The "clink" of the chisel against stone was music to his ears.

"Adam! I need you to take out the garbage!" his mother yelled.

"In a minute!" he yelled back. Silence followed, and Adam relaxed. But a second later, his mother came through the garage door and stood before him, arms crossed and lips pursed.

"Not 'in a minute,'" she said. "Now. You have been saying 'in a minute' for the last hour. You will take the garbage out now."

Adam let out a very audible sigh to show his discontent. "But I am right in the middle of something," he argued. "I can see it in my head right now, and I don't want to lose it!" His mother didn't answer. She just stood and stared.

"Fine," he said and dropped the chisel on the workbench to accentuate his unhappiness, and then went into the house to gather wastebaskets. His mother followed. Adam continued to mutter as he went from room to room. Not until the cans were at the curb ready for pick up did he begin to feel a little foolish. His mother really shouldn't have had to remind him. It was his job and an easy chore to remember.

He returned to the garage and his bear. The head was beginning to take shape. He felt himself relax. He had all weekend so why had he fought over fifteen minutes?

At dinner he took a break and joined the family. Dishes were his sister Denise's job so once dessert was finished, he asked to be excused.

"Don't forget you promised to help me with my math tonight," Denise said as he headed toward the back door. Adam stopped.

"That was tonight?" he asked. Denise nodded. "I –" he began, but knew he really couldn't make up an excuse to get out of it. His project wasn't due for over a month and so he had time. It's just that he wanted so much to work on the bear. He swallowed. "When do you want to do that?" he asked instead.

"Can we do it right after I do the dishes?" she asked and Adam nodded.

Now what? he thought. Denise would be ready in half an hour. That wouldn't allow him time to get anything really done. He turned back toward the table. "Let me help you then," he said, figuring that the sooner the dishes were done, the sooner they would get to the math, and the sooner he would get back to his sculpting.

Two hours later he was back in the garage, ironically feeling pleased rather than upset. Denise really struggled with math but was willing to work hard, and Adam felt a sense of achievement when he was able to explain the problem in a way that she understood. Even doing the dishes together had been kind of fun.

He worked on the sculpture for another two hours, relishing the sound of chisel against stone – Clink! Clink! – before he hit a snag. Something just wasn't right. Something wasn't looking the way it should, and he knew he couldn't really continue until he figured it out. Unlike oil painting, where an artist could fix a mistake, once the stone was cut, it was over. Mistakes were tough, if not impossible, to correct.

The situation frustrated him but he knew there was nothing he could do. If he continued, he could ruin the entire sculpture. But stopping work completely seemed like time wasted. He took a deep breath. He would have to take it back to school and have his art teacher advise him.

He fought the frustration but finally resigned himself to what had to be. Then a peace began to replace the anxiety.

This dilemma turned out to be a good thing, for Adam had forgotten that the family was spending all of Saturday at his grandparents.

On Monday morning Adam and the bear went straight to the art room. Mrs. Baker was already there. Adam explained his concern as Mrs. Baker looked at his burgeoning sculpture and smiled.

"You just need to chisel more away… here," she said pointing to a spot and from an angle Adam hadn't seen before. Once he had seen it through Mrs. Baker's eyes, it made perfect sense. His unwilling patience had paid off with new insight. Suddenly, the entire weekend came into new light.

God, too, was a sculptor – a master sculptor – and Adam was his stone.

Clink! Friday afternoon – the garbage – broken promises became renewed faithfulness.

Clink! Friday night – helping Denise – selfish desires became kindness.

Clink! Saturday and Sunday – the inability to continue sculpting – frustration became peace.

Clink! Clink! Clink! God had been chipping away at him for seventeen years already, but Adam knew the final work of art would not be complete or perfect until eternity itself.

Adam was sure God was speaking through Michelangelo when he had the artist proclaim that "In every block of marble I see a statue as plain as though it stood before me, shaped and perfect in attitude and action. I have only to hew away the rough walls that imprison… it."

And so does God, thought Adam smiling. *So does God. So chip away, Lord. Chip away.*

"I'm Not Hurting Anyone"

"You forgot to put your seatbelt on, Cassie."

"I don't want to," came the reply.

Jayden looked at her older sister, confused.

"But I thought it was the law?" she said.

Cassie was silent for a moment, started to reply, then stopped, looked at her ten-year-old sister, pursed her lips, and then finally answered.

"Well, it is, but I think it's a stupid law. People should be able to decide if they want to wear their seatbelt or not. This shoulder strap just isn't comfortable. You don't want me to be uncomfortable do you?" she asked. "And anyway, it's not like I'm hurting anyone."

Cassie could see her sister's brow furrow in deeper thought.

"But if the police stop you, you'll still get a ticket, right? Even if you think it's a stupid rule?" Jayden asked.

"I'm not going to get a ticket," Cassie stated flatly, but Jayden wasn't letting up.

"So, people don't have to follow the rules if the rules make them uncomfortable?" she asked.

Cassie sighed. That wasn't it at all. Why did Jayden ask so many questions? She was missing the point. But Cassie was at a loss as to how to explain what the point really was, or how it would make sense because no matter how she tried to answer, it wasn't sounding right.

Maybe because it isn't right, a silent voice whispered, and Cassie's exasperation grew.

Meanwhile, Jayden kept the pressure coming. "And anyway, I would rather you be safe than happy. Aren't you supposed to wear your seatbelt to keep you safe?" she asked.

"Don't worry. I'm a safe driver. Nothing's going to happen."

"But you don't know that, Cassie."

"Well, if something does happen, the only one hurt will be me. You *have* your seatbelt on."

That was not the reassuring answer Jayden wanted. "But if something happens to you then it *will* hurt me!" Jayden almost yelled, tears forming in her eyes. "I don't want anything to happen to you!"

Cassie let out another deep sigh, tired of the argument that was getting more convoluted by the minute.

"Nothing will happen," she said, hoping that would put the issue at rest.

But Jayden just sat back in her seat distraught.

"I just don't get it, then," she said, still almost in tears. "Why have the rules if people don't think they have to follow them? It is really confusing."

"Well, maybe one day when you start driving, you'll understand," Cassie replied condescendingly.

The two arrived home without incident.

"Seeeeee," Cassie said when she shut off the engine. "Nothing happened."

Jayden wasn't mollified. She was not reassured. "This time," was all she said and climbed out of the car.

Dinner was a tense time for Cassie as she waited for Jayden to spill the beans about the seatbelt, but Jayden's mind and conversation had moved on to more important things – namely a birthday party on Saturday – and Cassie could feel herself relaxing.

Good, she thought. *That's over.* She settled down to watch a little TV. After clicking through a couple of stations, she landed on an interview with a popular young actress. After questions about her career and next project, the interview turned more personal.

"I hear you and your boyfriend are looking to start a family," the host said and the actress nodded.

Cassie was shaking her head. *She could be getting herself into a lot of trouble,* she thought. *After all, how many Hollywood couples stay together even* after *they marry.*

"What do you think your fans will say?" the host asked.

"After all, you have been known to have very high morals and some will see this as a departure. You also profess to believe the Bible after all."

The actress smiled. "I do believe the Bible," she answered, "but some parts are a bit archaic and so really don't apply to today."

"So does thinking those standards don't apply exempt you from the consequences?" he asked.

"There aren't going to be any consequences," came the response, this time laced with a bit of irritation. "Besides, what could be so wrong if we are so in love and happy. After all, the Bible is all about love, right? Do people really not want us to be happy?"

"I see," came the reply, intentionally avoiding casting a vote.

Cassie could feel her skin grow a bit clammy and her mouth turn a bit dry. These arguments were sounding oddly familiar.

"And besides, I'm not hurting anyone else. If something happens the only person hurt will be me."

And your child! Cassie wanted to scream. The host avoided that obvious omission too but carried on.

"Don't you think you are sending out mixed messages?" he asked. "You believe the Bible but you don't follow it? That could be a little confusing for your fans, especially your young fans." The actress's smile was quite a bit tighter this time.

"Well, when they get older and fall in love, then they will understand," she said, and it was obvious that she wanted no more of this conversation.

Cassie turned the TV off and stared at the wall. Her little departure from following the seatbelt law had caused all sorts of confusion in Jayden. True, no one was hurt physically, but if every older sister did as she had done, and if every younger ten-year-old sister was as confused as Jayden, then six years "down the road" who knew how the seatbelt law might be viewed: optional, stupid, an intrusion into a person's life and happiness?

And that was just a seatbelt law. How much more damage would be done by manipulating or ignoring God's laws in the name of happiness and personal rights? The statement "I'm not hurting anyone" was a complete lie. Actions have consequences beyond the individuals involved. *Everyone* is hurt because when lines are blurred and accountability is forgotten, confusion and discord reign, which is just what Satan wants. Satan is the author of confusion while God is the author of peace.

God's laws are not put in place to make life miserable but to give us life and give it more abundantly (John 10:10). Following God's laws at first may not seem to cater to a person's immediate happiness or comfort, but it *will* bring lasting peace and joy.

Under the Hood

Jose just stared at the car before him, and his stomach gave an uneasy flip flop. *So this is what $1000 buys,* he thought sadly, swallowed hard, and began a slow walk around the car while the owner eyed him suspiciously. *Is he afraid I'm going to steal it?* he wondered. *He could only hope.*

The paint job, or what was left of it, was pathetic. It had started as a royal blue, but the years (and there were plenty of them) had been harsh. The paint was either in the process of peeling or had already done so, leaving exposed primer, or worse, rust.

One of the back taillights had been broken and there was red cellophane duct taped in place. Jose licked his lips. The lock on the trunk had been punched out and the lid was being held in place by wire. To top it off, the passenger side mirror was missing.

Jose's spirits sunk to his stomach. Dare he look inside? With trepidation he moved closer and peered through the window. Just as he thought. It was in shambles. The upholstery had to be the original vinyl—cracked and ripped. Some duct tape had been strategically placed to hide the bigger rips. Jose calculated that an entire roll had been used and *still* there were open wounds. The headliner wasn't much better and, in fact, was loose along the edges.

Jose stepped back from the car and let out a despondent sigh. To top it off, it wasn't even a respectable Hispanic car, like a Chevy Impala or a Monte Carlo or better yet, a Chevy Camaro. At least one of those vintage cars would have some staying power while he tried to fix it up. Nope. This was a Ford – and to make it worse, it was a 1978 Ford Zephyr. Nothing classic or sporty or… well, anything. In its day it might have been his grandmother's car. No self-respecting girl would want to ride with him in *this*.

Jose sighed again.

"Don't do it, Jose! Don't even think about it!"

Jose's head popped up, and he looked toward the street where Santiago and Tomas were riding by in Santiago's tripped out Impala. The two were shaking their heads and laughing at him.

"You will lose all your street cred, man, if you buy that piece of junk," Tomas called out, and Jose turned to look at the owner, embarrassed by the outcry from his friends.

"Sorry," he apologized, as the two drove on.

"Doesn't bother me," the man said. "What do you think? Are you interested?"

Jose's shoulders rose and fell with another heavy sigh. What was he thinking even considering this car? It was a junker, pure and simple.

"Can I see under the hood?" he asked, and he swore he saw the man's mouth twitch.

"You sure?" he asked, and Jose nodded. Now a slight smile became visible as the man moved to open the hood. Jose stood back until the hood was secure and then moved up to take a look. What he saw caught him completely off guard. He moved in closer and then went from one side of the car to the other.

The engine compartment was spotless, and the engine shone brightly. While the outside of the car showed its age, the part hidden under the hood looked brand new.

"Is that a –" he was at a loss for words but looked up at the owner, the smile that had been twitching at the corners of his mouth was now just itching to get out.

"A what?" the man asked, curious if Jose really *did* know what he was looking at.

Jose swallowed hard. "Is that a 1968 BMW AG Inline 6?"

Now the man smiled broadly. "So you know your engines," he said.

"I know that *that* engine costs a whole lot more than what you're asking for *this* car," Jose replied. "A whole lot more. Why hasn't anyone bought it yet?"

"Why do you think?" the man asked. "No one gets past the exterior to even want to take a look at what's under the hood.

Jose nodded slowly in understanding. *He* almost didn't look under the hood. In fact, if he had had a dime more than the $1,000 to spend on a car, he wouldn't have given this car a second look either. Now, all of a sudden, the paint didn't look that bad, the upholstery was usable, and the minor flaws were just that – minor and fixable. Even it being a 1978 Ford Zephyr, undoubtedly one of Ford's ugliest models, didn't make a difference anymore. Once the guys knew what he had, he would be the envy of everyone.

"Well, you know I am going to take it," he said to the man, and then got a painful realization. "That is if you aren't changing the price on me now that I know about the engine."

Still smiling, the man shook his head. "I can't do that," he stated. "One thousand was the published asking price and that's what it will stay. I am just elated it will be going to someone who appreciates it. This little car has served me well."

Jose counted out the ten crisp $100 bills that he had just pulled from the bank into the man's hand after which the man signed and handed over the pink slip.

Jose couldn't believe his good fortune, and then another bit of reality hit him. How many other times had he missed a hidden treasure because he was only focused on the outside? Not just with a car, but with a situation or a person. How many situations had he complained about because they weren't going his way when he might have missed the buried treasure God wanted him to find? Or what about people? So concerned was he and every other guy he knew about what a girl looked like that they had probably missed another of God's hidden gems. And how much more concerned was he with his own looks than he was with his own inner being… the shape of his own motor.

He took the keys and on the spot he made a promise to himself and to God. Each improvement he made on the car's exterior would be matched by an improvement of his own interior. This car would be his reminder from God on what really matters – what's under the hood.

Employee of the Month

"Guess who just got hired here," Nicole whispered to Amy, almost giddy with excitement. "Barry McDonald!"

Amy's reaction did not disappoint Nicole. Her eyes grew to hubcap size and her mouth opened wide enough to entrap seven tunas.

"No! When does he start?" she whispered back.

"Today!"

The two looked at each other and then squealed in delight. Billy glanced over as he continued to load a super pepperoni and sausage with another layer of pepperoni. Despite all the "whispering," he had heard every word of the conversation.

Girls! he thought. *Why do they get all gaga over some football player? So what if the guy is six-three, weighs a solid one-eighty, is built like a tank, and has a Tom Cruise smile? What's the big deal?*

Nicole and Amy had forgotten all about making pizzas

and were instead deep in conversation about the possibility that their shift just might overlap Barry's on his first night and then that the manager just might have enough insight and compassion to always schedule them with Barry. Billy thought momentarily that perhaps he should remind them that customers were waiting, but he held his tongue. That was the manager's role. Instead, he slid his finished pizza into the oven and then reached over and grabbed the order in front of Nicole. She didn't even notice.

Sometime between then and the arrival of "Mr." McDonald, the manager did notice that Nicole and Amy had ceased any productive work, and she sent both girls home. They begged to stay, but the manager said she had already lost two hours wages on each of them and wasn't going to lose any more. The girls couldn't believe it.

Their departure really didn't leave Billy and the others with any extra work (since they were doing it all anyway), but it did give them a much quieter working environment. That is until Barry McDonald walked in. Then, a hush fell over the pizza parlor as every head popped up, regardless of age, and the whispering began again. See, Barry McDonald is the closest thing to a sports hero that Millville has ever had. The college football offers had been pouring in. Other small California towns had their football heroes – Clovis had Darryl Lamonica, Sanger had Tom Flores, Chico had Aaron Rodgers – and now Millville had Barry McDonald.

Billy didn't notice the change in the atmosphere at first because he was so busy in the back cutting up onions and tomatoes. But when he brought the new bins out, he noticed the eerie difference and looked around. There was Barry McDonald, big as life, in a Piping Hot Pizza shirt and hat like the rest of them.

The manager brought Barry back and presented him to Billy.

"Billy, I want you to show Barry everything there is to know about making a Piping Hot Pizza," she said and then left.

Billy knew Barry by reputation only and had never stood closer than ten feet to him. It almost put a crick in his neck to look him in the eye. He grinned up at the football god.

"Don't worry," he said, tongue in cheek, "all you need to know will take up only about a milligram of brain space."

Barry grinned and wiped his forehead with the back of his hand in mock relief.

"Phew," he said. "I was afraid I would have to throw out a few plays from the playbook to make room. You know the stories about a jock's brain."

Billy laughed. This guy was all right.

Barry was a quick learner. He didn't forget anything, and he was always looking for something to keep busy. When the three o'clock lull hit, he sought Billy out.

"The tables are all clean and there aren't any customers.

What do you do now?"

"Things start picking up again around four and then the big rush starts at five," Billy said. "After that, there's not much time to play catch up, so why don't we make sure we have two bins of everything in the refrigerator ready to go."

Barry nodded and followed Billy. The two of them began cutting onions, mushrooms, and tomatoes and filling bins with other pizza toppings. The manager popped her head in to see how they were doing. She smiled when she saw them working away. Billy and Barry never even noticed she was there.

. . .

Barry had been working almost three weeks when the monthly employees' meeting was held. In that time, business had picked up tremendously, and all because of Barry.

Word had gotten out that Millville's finest was working at the Piping Hot Pizza Parlor and suddenly all of Millville wanted pizza and a little slice of "their man." Billy didn't resent it at all. After all, Barry was a great worker, and he was even greater with the public.

If he had a lull in his job, he would cruise the dining area, wiping up little spills, asking people if they needed anything, and just chatting. He knew what the people came for, and he was willing to oblige. Billy was amazed he could take all the attention without it affecting his personality at all, but he did and it didn't. He was genuinely a nice guy, and the two were getting to be pretty good friends. Barry still came to Billy whenever he had a question.

Another reason Billy didn't resent Barry was because the manager, in her infinite wisdom, had made sure that Nicole and Amy never shared a shift with the football god. When justice is served, one can't complain. So the employees' meeting was the first time Nicole and Amy found themselves in close proximity to Barry, and they were drooling all over themselves before the meeting ever began.

After an hour of discussion about procedure changes and new menu items, the manager switched gears.

"This month we have seen a drastic increase in business, which is good," she said. "But often, such a drastic increase causes some confusion and chaos and therefore a decrease in productivity and customer satisfaction. That didn't happen this time because of one person."

All eyes shifted toward Barry. Everyone knew where this was headed.

"This person, I have discovered," the manager continued, "has proven himself invaluable to Piping Hot Pizza. He is efficient; generous with his time; a good, faithful worker; and extremely helpful to others."

Everyone was nodding, grinning, and staring straight at Barry, who hadn't blinked an eye and seemed totally unaware of all the attention he was getting.

"This month's Employee of the Month goes to"– she paused for dramatic effect –"Billy Meyer."

It took a moment for the name to register with everyone, especially Billy. Only Barry didn't seem shocked. He was on his feet in a minute clapping wildly and yelling, "That's my man!"

Pen Pals

"**B**ailey, Virginia. First Row. Third Seat. Barker, Tricia. First row. Fourth seat."

Tricia silently groaned as she moved to her assigned seat. *So this year wasn't going to be much different,* she mused. It was only third period, and this was the second class in which she was forced to sit behind Virginia Bailey. Why did teachers have to have such predictable seating charts?

As luck would have it, Virginia's ally, John Castro, drew the seat right next to Tricia. No sooner had John taken his seat than the two started their incessant gossiping.

Memories of last year came flooding back. For four periods, Tricia had listened to Virginia's threats and questionable exploits. Tricia looked at her furtively. Virginia was pretty with her long blonde hair, clear blue eyes, and soft complexion. Bur her pent-up anger was predominant.

"Please take out a pen and a piece of paper," Mrs. Patterson directed once everyone had been seated.

Tricia opened her binder.

"What if you don't have one?" Virginia asked with mock innocence. "Didn't think we'd need one the first day."

Tricia's heart stopped. In her pencil pouch were twenty pens with Scripture verses on them. This summer her Sunday school class had decided to meet needs while witnessing, hence the pens, since every student needed one at one time or another. At the time Tricia had embraced the idea. Being moderately shy, she had always balked at sharing her faith. This seemed such an easy way out. Just slip someone a pen and then slip out of the picture. But in her visions, the person had always been some withdrawn loner in need of a friend, not Virginia.

Somehow Tricia managed to extract a pen from the case and hand it to Virginia, verse-side down. Hesitantly she heard herself say, "I have a pen you can have."

Virginia turned to look at her in disbelief.

"I don't need your stupid pen," she said disgustedly. She looked at John with a can-you-believe-this look, and took a pencil from him.

Tricia slowly retracted the pen and prayed for the earth to swallow her up. The rest of the day went better since her last three classes were without Virginia.

That night while in her room organizing her notebook, she saw the pens. For a long time she toyed with the idea of conveniently leaving them at home. But she knew it was a cop-out.

"Okay, Lord," she prayed quietly. "You win. But give me the strength and courage to handle this situation." She paused and smiled slightly. "Better yet, please let Virginia remember her own pen tomorrow."

But Virginia didn't. For a week, Virginia vocalized her plight, much to the teacher's dismay and Virginia's delight. And for a week, Tricia gritted her teeth and offered her a pen. The response was always the same. For a while, Mrs. Patterson accepted her work in pencil, but finally she put her foot down.

"Virginia, I've given you time to secure a pen. I will no longer accept your work in pencil." She addressed the class. "Does anyone have a pen Virginia can use?"

"I do," Tricia answered.

"Thank you, Tricia. Virginia, I suggest you take it."

Virginia turned around with dramatic indignation and begrudgingly took the pen – a red one. Tricia held her breath and waited for Virginia to read the inscription and say something crude. But no comment came. *Maybe she hasn't read it yet,* thought Tricia. She spent an uneasy forty-five minutes until the bell finally rang.

She went home that day feeling rather proud of herself but still apprehensive about Virginia's reaction. The next day, as usual, Virginia entered spouting off a list of recent accomplishments before plopping in her seat. Tricia waited. Nothing.

"Please take out a pen and some paper," directed Mrs. Patterson.

"I don't have a pen," Virginia responded.

Tricia's mouth dropped. *What?* she thought. *How could she have lost that pen already?* Before Mrs. Patterson could respond, Tricia said, "I have another one she can use," and Virginia spun around with her hand extended. Without a word of thanks she took the bright yellow pen and turned back around. Again Tricia cringed, waiting for Virginia's reaction. Again nothing.

This pattern continued for the rest of the week. Despite the fact that Tricia would give her a pen every day, Virginia would always claim she needed one. Finally, Tricia started leaving one at the top of her desk and Virginia would invariably pick it up. By the end of the third week, Virginia had depleted Tricia's supply, and at Sunday school she had to ask for more.

"My, you must be busy," Mr. Morton, her teacher, said proudly. "Take as many as you like."

Tricia blushed, mumbled a quick "yes" and "thank you," and grabbed a handful. She didn't have the heart to tell him that they were all going to the same person.

Monday brought the same scenario. But at lunch, as Tricia walked toward her locker to deposit her books, she heard her name called.

"Hey! Barker!"

Tricia jumped, not used to being addressed by her last name. She turned around to see Virginia standing by the drinking fountain. Tricia shivered slightly, wondering if

Virginia had finally taken offense to the verses. She tried to calm herself.

"Yes?" she answered.

"Come 'ere," Virginia responded, motioning with her head.

Heart still pounding, Tricia approached her. "Uh huh?"

"Got any more of those pens?" she asked.

Tricia stared at her in disbelief, stifling an urge to ask her not only where the pen she just gave her was, but where the last thirty were. Instead she nodded. "Sure."

She opened her binder, unzipped the pouch, and pulled out three pens. "Here you go," she said as she handed them to her and turned to leave.

Virginia looked at them quickly then called after her.

"I already have these!"

Tricia stopped and turned around. "What?" she asked.

Virginia looked straight at her. "I said," she said slowly, "I already got these. What else do you have?"

"Uh," Tricia stammered. "Uh, well. Why don't you look?" she offered and held her binder open.

As Virginia intently read each pen before taking or discarding it, Tricia pieced the puzzle together. *Virginia hadn't lost all those pens,* she realized. *She was just collecting them to read.*

"You're missing one," she said.

"What?" Tricia asked again. "One what?"

"One of your pens," Virginia replied. "You had one that

said, 'Let not your heart be troubled' or something like that. It was the first one you gave me, but I lost it. Do you have any more of those?"

Tricia felt somewhat embarrassed. She hadn't bothered to read any of them. Quickly she fumbled through the pouch.

"There aren't any in there," Virginia said impatiently. "I already checked."

"Uh, I'm sorry," Tricia stuttered. "I could get one for you, but it might take a week."

Virginia's face furrowed as she thought about the offer. "A week, huh?" She paused. "Well, okay. Though I'm kind of in a hurry to know how to do that."

"Do what?" asked Tricia. The whole situation had caught her off guard.

"Not be troubled!" Virginia repeated impatiently.

"Sorry," apologized Tricia. She caught her breath and prayed silently before continuing.

"Say Virginia," she began, scarcely able to hear her own voice over the pounding of her heart. "Would you like the entire book that all those sayings come from? I could have that to you by tomorrow."

Virginia pursed her lips and thought a moment. "Tomorrow, huh? Okay. But I still want that pen."

"Sure," Tricia agreed.

"Okay," Virginia agreed and Tricia watched as Virginia walked off without so much as a thank you. She could give Virginia one of her Bibles and put a marker at the verses written on the pens. With Virginia gone, Tricia finally relaxed. She didn't know how Virginia would react when she handed her a Bible tomorrow, but that was tomorrow's worry, not today's. At any rate, God seemed to have everything very much under His control and the seeds were planted. Tricia stopped, thought about it, and then corrected herself. *Make that pens!*

A Good Friend Would

He kept saying, 'if… if you love me, you… you'll do it. If you… you love me.' And all I could think was… that if I didn't do it,… that he… that he would dump me. Now just look what's happened. I… I don't know what I'm going to do."

I listened in shocked silence as Melinda recounted her dilemma through racking sobs and hiccups. Before I could think of anything to say, Melinda continued, her voice a little more under control.

"Jessie, you've just got to help me," she pleaded.

"Sure," I responded quickly, grateful for an easy answer. "How?"

"I've got to get an abortion, fast," she said.

I felt the blood freeze in my veins. *What was I getting into?*

"What did you want me to do?" I asked weakly and closed my eyes, dreading her answer.

"Your dad's a doctor," she said, and it was incredible how calm her voice suddenly sounded. "Feel him out for a doctor who will give me an abortion without my parent's knowing, and let me know how much it will cost."

I sat silent, numb all over. "I don't know if I can," I said softly. And that was the truth. As a Christian, I was adamantly pro-life.

But that stand had never been tested like it was being tested today.

"You have to," she pleaded.

"But Melinda," I argued, knowing I didn't sound very convincing. "Maybe abortion isn't the right choice. Maybe you should talk to your parents." My pro-life stand was stuck somewhere between my yellow back and my throat.

"I can't tell my parents!" she yelled back. "Never! And you better not say anything to anybody either. You're the only person who knows about this."

I sat taken aback and a bit flustered by her outburst, but I wasn't ready to give in yet.

"I won't, but I don't know, Melinda, I –" I didn't have time to finish.

"A *good* friend wouldn't be wavering like this," she said irately. "A *good* friend would help."

I felt lost and on the defensive, and I wanted to get out of this conversation as quickly as possible.

"All right," I said. "I'll see what I can do."

"Great," Melinda replied sweetly. "I knew I could count on you."

I hung up the phone and lay back on my bed staring up at the ceiling. *What have I gotten myself into?* I wondered and tried to figure a way to work the needed information out of my father without raising any suspicion. I decided on a casual conversation during dinner.

• • •

"Dad, Mrs. Sylvester, our biology teacher, wondered if you would know of a doctor who would be willing to come to our school and talk about abortion," I asked casually. Everyone's fork stopped in midair, and for my family, that's a major feat. I felt my own wedge of meatloaf threatening to make a re-appearance and wanted to slide into the depths of the earth right then.

"When did she start bringing in doctors?" Stephanie, my older sister, asked. "She never brought them into class when I had her. In fact, I don't even remember studying abortion in biology."

I felt my blood rise to my face. *Why hadn't I thought this approach through more?* I chided myself. *Now I was about to be caught in the thick of it.*

"It's something new," I lied again. Stephanie eyed me closer, and I just knew she was on to something. But before she had a chance to pounce, Dad spoke up.

"No, I'm afraid I won't, Jessie," he answered firmly. "You know how I feel about abortion, and I won't be a party to perhaps encouraging some young lady to have one. If you like, I'll call Mrs. Sylvester and explain my concerns to her. Maybe we can work something out."

"No!" I answered much too quickly, and Stephanie gave me another skeptical look. "It's OK, Dad," I hurried on, trying to look like I was really in control. "It's no big deal. She just said to ask. No problem. Really."

He went back to eating but wasn't quite satisfied. My request had disrupted his digestive rhythm. "Maybe I should just call down there anyway, find out exactly what they're trying to teach you. As a parent I have that right, you know."

I thought I was going to die.

"Oh, please don't, Dad," I begged. "I just said I was going to ask. Don't make a federal case out of it. I would just die."

Dad chewed his meatloaf slowly, stared at me, and then glanced at Mom, who shook her head slowly.

"Too much, huh?" he asked her, and she nodded. "OK," he agreed. "But you'll fill me in on what she covers?"

I nodded anxiously, and he grunted and went back to his meatloaf. My whole body wilted with relief. I had escaped one major catastrophe, but that still left me with another. What was I going to tell Melinda? I let out a long sigh, looked up right into Stephanie's steady, penetrating eyes, and my whole body tensed. I forgot about eating and excused myself.

• • •

"Jessie! It's for you!"

"I'll get it in here!" I yelled back and picked up the receiver. It was Melinda.

"Well?" she asked anxiously. "Did you find out anything?"

I stalled, not knowing what to do. "I can't get a name," I blurted, then closed my eyes and waited. Silence filled the line for what seemed like an hour.

"Great," she finally said. "Some friend you turned out to be."

"Melinda," I argued. "I tried. It's just my dad wasn't about to give out any information without knowing every detail, and you didn't want me to say anything."

"Forget it," she snapped. "I'll find out myself. How about lending me a little money then? You're dad's a doctor. You've got plenty around there. Surely, you can lend me some. That's not too tough, is it?"

There was no missing the sarcasm in her voice, and I licked my dry lips before replying.

"Melinda, I don't have that kind of money." I spoke quickly, trying to get it all out before she could say anything. "I only get an allowance, and if I ask them for more, they're going to want to know why, and –"

"Then lie!" she almost screamed. "Man, what kind of friend are you? A *good* friend would help!" And she slammed down the receiver.

I dropped the receiver on the hook and flopped back on my bed feeling completely lost as to what to do. My first lie had alienated me from my parents. And I already knew where God stood on the issue, so there was really no reason to ask Him. I rolled over and buried my head in my pillow. *Why me?* I moaned to myself. A gentle knock sounded at my door.

"Yeah?" I said cautiously and waited.

The door opened, and Stephanie poked her head in. My body went numb.

"Can I come in?" she asked smiling slightly.

I eyed her carefully, afraid yet a little grateful for some company.

"Sure," I said as I sat up on my bed and pulled my knees to my chest. Stephanie sat on the end of the bed and stared at the floor, obviously trying to determine the best way to start. She opted for the blunt approach.

"Jessie, are you in trouble?" she asked with concern.

"What?" I responded, a little unsure of what I had heard.

"Are you pregnant?" she asked straightforward.

I couldn't help but laugh.

"No."

"Is a friend of yours?"

I didn't laugh this time. I didn't say anything. I didn't have to. Stephanie had figured it out.

"Did she put you up to asking Dad?" she continued.

I licked my lips, thought about my promise not to say anything, figured I really wasn't, and nodded. Stephanie sighed and pursed her lips.

"Anything else?" she asked after a moment.

"She wants some money," I answered, and Stephanie's eyebrows rose.

"Are you going to give it to her?" she asked, and I plopped over on the bed.

"I don't know," I answered truthfully. "I feel so sorry for her." Then I went on to tell her Melinda's whole plight, without ever revealing the name, of course. "And then she kept saying, 'A *good* friend would,' and now I don't know what to do."

"Sounds like she is using the same line on you that her boyfriend used on her, with a slight variation," Stephanie stated, and I could tell she was upset. "If you get my drift." I nodded.

"And by the way," she continued and looked me straight in the eye. "While we're on the subject of good friends, a *good* friend would never have asked you to do that in the first place!"

The Toughest Challenge

Alan stepped on the scales and anxiously watched the needle rise to 144 1/2. He smiled. He had made his weight with half a pound to spare. He watched as the official made a notation on his clipboard before stepping down.

"Next," said the official methodically, and up stepped another wrestler. Alan pulled on his sweats and then joined his teammates grouped together by the locker-room door.

"No problem, eh Alan?" joked Richie, their heavyweight, who never had to worry about making weight. "Don't see why you guys are always *sweating* over this." The others laughed at his pun.

"Speaking of sweating," said Mark, the senior 175 pounder, "has anyone seen John? He went out running an hour ago. Still had to drop three pounds."

They all laughed. "Yeah, I saw him about fifteen minute ago," Bob, a 119 sophomore answered. "He was still running."

"Well, he'd better hurry up," Jim insisted. "He has only a couple of more minutes to weigh in, and Coach will be pretty ticked if he's disqualified from the sectionals."

"There he is," yelled Gary, the 98 pounder, spotting John at the end of the line. The group moved toward the scales. They watched as wrestler after wrestler stepped on and off the scales. Finally, it was John's turn. The team held its collective breath as he stepped up. The needle fluctuated dramatically, and the official moved in closer to take a better reading. So did the team.

"One hundred sixty-five," barked the official and then under his breath muttered, "barely."

The team let out a cheer, and John breathed a sigh of relief and then, smiling, joined them.

"Wasn't worried a bit," he said nonchalantly, then rolled his eyes and feigned passing out.

Everyone laughed, then Richie addressed the group. "Well, troops, are we still on for tonight?"

A collective, "Yeah!" with raised fists was the reply. Alan looked somewhat puzzled.

"What's tonight?" he asked.

"Say, that's right," said Richie. "You're our new boy, aren't you? Keep forgetting this is your first year on the team. Well then, let me tell ya," Richie continued, placing his huge hand on Alan's shoulder in a brotherly fashion.

"Every year after we win the league championship–

like we did again this year... He paused looking expectantly about the group.

They answered with a hearty, "Yeah!"

"We get together on the eve of the sectional title to bond as a team. Tonight it's at my place. You get there about seven, then we have a few munchies, watch a couple of adrenaline boosting movies like *Rocky I, II, III,* or *IV,* to pump us up for tomorrow, and then we go home. It's a great time." He gave Alan an affectionate pat. "So how 'bout it? You'll be there, won't ya?"

Alan felt a warm glow course through his body. This had been a great season for him personally, and he felt even better now knowing that all the guys accepted him.

"Sure," he said enthusiastically. "Does Coach come?"

A titter of laughter rippled through the group, eyes catching eyes. Alan wondered uncomfortably what he had said that was so funny. He looked at Mark. Mark's face had turned red, and he wasn't smiling. But before Alan had a chance to ask anything, Richie patted him on the back and continued.

"Naw, Coach likes us to take the leadership role every once in a while, and this is one of those times. So it's just us guys for tonight, OK?"

Alan glanced about the smiling group and relaxed, but he couldn't help noticing Mark looking away. He wondered what was wrong with him.

"OK," he answered, and the group broke up. Alan

saw Mark leaving by the side door but didn't have a chance to question him before he was gone. Oh well, he'd follow up on it tonight.

Richie's house was only a couple of blocks from Alan's, so he decided to walk. The night was clear and crisp giving Alan a fresh surge of energy. Everything was going great. By the time he arrived, most of the other guys were already there munching on the chips or sandwiches that Mrs. Martin, Richie's mom, had made. Alan followed Richie into the family room and looked around.

"Where are your folks?" he asked. His question caused a few team members to look his way, but Richie fielded the question flawlessly.

"Went to see my grandparents. Figured three plus hours of Sly Stallone and hyper guys might get on their nerves.

Alan grinned. They were probably right. Mark showed up soon after, but looked extremely uncomfortable and for some reason seemed to be avoiding Alan. When Alan finally did corner him, Mark had little to say.

"Are you OK?" Alan asked.

"Yeah. I'm fine," he answered. "Just a little tense about tomorrow." Then he walked away.

Strange, thought Alan. He had felt pretty close to Mark all season. Both were Christians and attended the same church. Mark, who had wrestled for three years, had shared with Alan how he had learned to use the wrestling mat as a place to demonstrate his Christian faith. There wasn't anyone Alan admired more than Mark, and his sudden aloofness bothered him. But he respected the guy's privacy and didn't push the issue. Instead, he gave a silent prayer. *Take care of him, Lord. Help him through what's bothering him, and use me in any way you can.*

At seven thirty, the first of two Rocky films went in. They guys clamored around the TV, parroting the lines and calling for "Aaadrian." It was a great time of team oneness. Then between the first and second flick, Richie stood up and went to the kitchen, soon to return with a huge paper bag. Everyone sat smiling and looking at him expectantly.

"Now," he said as dramatically as he could. "It is time to toast the greatest high school wrestling team in the state."

"Oo-oo-oo-oo!" chanted the team, pumping their fists.

"A toast!" Richie yelled as he reached into the bag and began tossing a can to each guy. Alan caught the one aimed at him but wasn't sure if it was the coldness of the can or its contents that shot a sudden chill through his body. He looked at it cautiously and his mouth went dry. Then as tops popped and hoots went up around him, he looked up. He caught Mark eyeing him furtively, and when Mark saw the shock on Alan's face, his lips tightened and he looked away sadly. Alan was in turmoil. This was illegal. Not only because they had signed a code of ethics, but because they were under age. They could lose everything they had worked for.

His heart pounded. What should he do? As a Christian he knew he should stand up and do what was right, but he didn't want to. They had finally accepted him. What would they think now? He licked his lips – his heart pounding in his ears. He felt his mouth moving, but his voice seemed miles away.

"I don't think we should do this," his voice cracked. A hush followed as fifteen pairs of eyes settled on him. "What if we get caught?"

"Haven't yet," snickered Richie, grinning and taking a big swig. The others relaxed then as they laughed and took swigs of their own.

Alan didn't know what to do. He had no pull with this group. They would only laugh at him. He looked at Mark who was sitting mutely on the bar stool holding his open can of beer, and Alan's ire rose. This was *his* fourth year. Had he been a part of this for the past three? This guy who claimed to wrestle for Christ on the mat wasn't even willing to stand up for Him in someone's family room. Mark should be taking the lead here, standing up for what was right. His anger grew as he rose slowly, trying to regain his composure. The others looked at him.

"Hey, new boy's got a toast to make," said John, and the others cheered.

Alan looked at them slowly, stopping at Mark. "No…

no toast," he said softly and looked back at the others. "I just stood up to say I'm leaving. Not only are we underage, but we specifically signed a code of ethics saying we were willing to demand and expect more of ourselves than others. I don't know about you guys, but I take my oaths seriously."

The place had grown deathly quiet. He continued, "This can't help us a bit, only hurt us. I'm sorry, but I'll have no part of it." Then he turned to leave.

"Squeal and we'll implicate you," Richie said slowly, and Alan looked at him in disbelief.

"No, you won't," came a voice from a far bar stool, and Alan saw Mark stand up and lay his beer on the counter. "'Cause I'll vouch for him. Oh, you can say I was involved because for three years I've compromised and drank with you. But Alan's right. It's wrong, and I've been a hypocrite. I'm leaving too."

Alan looked at Mark gratefully, and his faltering admiration for the senior wrestler seemed to regain its footing. A few of the guys laid their beer cans down, and the raucous mood of the evening was dampened. But whether or not anyone else left, Alan and Mark didn't know. They didn't stay to watch. For them, the party was over.

Peace on Earth?

"**G**et out! Now!"

Jimmy stared at his father, his face stinging, his eyes watering, his anger building.

"Did you hear me?!" his father yelled. "Get out now before I slug you again!"

Jimmy looked at his crying mother, her eyes pleading with him. Seven-year-old Britney and ten-year-old Michael Jr. huddled in fear behind the couch. Jimmy's father took another step toward him, and Jimmy, overwhelmed by the stench of alcohol and sweat, grabbed his coat and was out the door, leaving the chaos behind him.

He walked as fast as he could until he was three blocks away. Then he slowed his pace and took a deep breath. The quiet enveloped him. Words and tears welled up inside him but he resisted the urge to swear. Swearing was as natural as breathing in his house, but as a new Christian, he knew swearing did nothing to remedy the situation and was dishonoring to God.

"Why does he have to ruin everything!" he finally said.

He looked up and down the street. Christmas lights twinkled, and through a window he could see a Christmas tree.

He felt a heavy sadness. There had been no Christmas tree at his house, which is what had started the fight. His mother had suggested they go down to the tree lot where they gave away leftover trees on Christmas Eve, but the suggestion had thrown his father into a rage. He wasn't about to accept charity. He had slapped his mother across the face, the red imprint of his hand appearing almost immediately. Without thinking, Jimmy had stepped in and pushed his father away. The next impact was for him, a full right cross that sent Jimmy sprawling. When he managed to get up, his father had demanded he get out.

But now what? he thought.

He took a deep breath. "Lord, I could sure use some of the 'peace on earth' tonight."

• • •

"Lord, make me an instrument of your peace tonight. May someone see your love and protection through me."

Officer James Keegan prayed those words every night before going on patrol. He was a rookie cop, who saw his role as a police officer as the perfect parallel of a loving heavenly father: protector and conveyer of justice and peace. Tonight, Christmas Eve, he felt a heightened sense of anticipation, for even though he was a bachelor, he had made himself a huge Christmas dinner with all the trimmings. Now four-fifths of it sat in his refrigerator. He could be eating turkey for a long time. Then there was the last of the Blue Santa gifts still in his trunk – a mixup at the station as shoppers had bought for one family twice, so the presents would sit in his trunk until it could be sorted out after the holidays.

"One Edward Four, ten-eight," James called in. He was now officially on duty.

"Roger that One Edward Four," came the reply.

• • •

Jimmy shivered. The chill of the evening air was settling in. His stomach rumbled, reminding him he hadn't eaten. He pulled his jacket tighter and prayed. Though hungry and cold, he knew there was more pressing business. The options churned inside him, but finally he felt a peace and his actions became clear. It wouldn't be easy, but it was the right thing to do. He took a deep breath, got his bearings, and headed down Main Street, his destination a couple of miles away.

• • •

Officer James Keegan started his patrol down Main Street, the police radio crackling in the background. Off to his right, he saw a walker, hunched over, bracing against the cold, and walking deliberately toward him. Curious, Keegan pulled over. Who would be out walking in this bitter cold? The walker approached the car.

• • •

Jimmy's heart caught. The patrol car saved him the two mile walk to the station but also meant he couldn't change his mind. When the passenger window rolled down and Jimmy stepped to the curb, relief washed over him. This was God's confirmation that he was doing the right thing, for behind the wheel was Officer Keegan, the man who helped out his youth group, the man who had led him to Christ.

"Jimmy!" Officer Keegan exclaimed. "What are you doing out in this cold? Get in."

Jimmy willingly obliged, shutting the door on the cold.

"What's going on?" Keegan asked.

Jimmy stared at his hands and took a deep breath. This wasn't easy.

"My father," he said. "He hit my mom."

Keegan let out a sigh. Michael Price was at it again—and on Christmas Eve no less. He shook his head.

"Jimmy," he said quietly. "You know when I get there, your mother won't press charges. And if she doesn't, then there isn't much I can do."

Jimmy continued to stare at his hands but when he looked up, in the dim light, Keegan could just detect some lividity on Jimmy's cheek.

"Jimmy?" he asked softly.

"He hit *me* this time," Jimmy said. "*I* want to press charges." He paused before continuing. "I figure if he is willing to hit me now, then it is only a matter of time before he might start on Mike Jr. or Britney."

Keegan nodded. He didn't tell Jimmy that it was unnecessary for him to press charges. Jimmy was a minor and Keegan was now obligated to report and investigate, but he knew the decision had been hard for Jimmy just the same. Keegan smiled weakly. This was indeed a bitter blessing. A young teen and his family were hurting, but they would at least have a peaceful Christmas Eve for once. He depressed his microphone.

"One Edward Four," he said. "Sarah, I'm taking Jimmy Price to my house for a minute while I go get his father. I'll explain when I get in. Then I'll take him home."

"Roger that One Edward Four."

As they drove toward Keegan's home he looked over at Jimmy.

"Jimmy, you need to know that God has had His hand in all this," he said.

Jimmy just looked at him. As a new Christian he wasn't used to seeing God in the middle of such chaos.

"How?"

"Oh, you'll see," he said with a slight smile. "Let's just say it involves quite a bit of turkey and a trunkful of presents."

Jimmy's stomach rumbled at the mention of turkey and he smiled at the thought of presents. Then another thought occurred to him.

"Do you think God could throw in a Christmas tree?"

Other books by J.E. Solinski

A Matter of Control

Five very different people wrestle with the ultimate question: Who is in control?

Martha Richards is a high school teacher who prides herself on her efficiency in the classroom and her ability to solve problems. Three of Martha's students—Reba Washington, Alex Kowalski, and Travis Richards—and Martha's own son, Danny, find themselves entangled in a web of best intentions that Martha creates and then tries to control. But her intervention brings unintended consequences for everyone.

In *A Matter of Control*, faith is tested and illusions are shattered as each of the five comes face to face with the truth of who is really in control.

• • •

Meet Charlie

Charlie Moynahan is happy that fourth grade is over and summer is underway... that is until a new kid, Rudy Roberts, moves into the neighborhood and disrupts Charlie's world.

However, when a robbery occurs around the corner at fellow fourth grader Sarah Morris's house, Charlie, with the help of best friend Harold Streeter, begins her own investigation, hoping not only to earn the reward money but also to put Rudy Roberts in his place.

Meet Charlie takes the reader on an adventurous journey of self-discovery as Charlie learns about prejudice, misunderstanding, friendship, and sacrifice.

Available through booksellers, Ingram, Amazon.com and jesolinski.com
Ask about our fundraising opportunities.

www.ingramcontent.com/pod-product-compliance
Lightning Source LLC
Chambersburg PA
CBHW031307120726
47906CB00003B/925